THE
COMBAT
ZONE

THE
COMBAT
ZONE

A CODY HARPER NOVEL

VINCENT WILDE

CLEiS
PRESS

Published in the United States by Cleis Press, an imprint of Start Midnight, LLC, 101 Hudson Street, Thirty-Seventh Floor, Suite 3705, Jersey City, NJ 07302.

Printed in the United States.
Cover design: Scott Idleman/Blink
Cover photograph: iStock
Text design: Frank Wiedemann

First Edition.
10 9 8 7 6 5 4 3 2 1

Trade paper ISBN: 978-1-62778-210-4
E-book ISBN: 978-1-62778-211-1

This novel is dedicated to the members of the LGBTQ community whose voices have been stilled by violence, and especially to Charlie Howard, a gay man beaten and thrown to his death from a bridge on July 7, 1984 in Bangor, Maine. The three teenagers arrested for Howard's death bragged to friends that they "jumped a fag and beat the shit out of him."

CHUCKAHOMO BRIDGE – BANGOR, MAINE

FLORIDA BIKER T-SHIRT, 1989

"...everything human has its origin in human weakness."

FRANZ STANGL – COMMANDANT OF TREBLINKA

CHAPTER ONE

BOSTON – 1995

The tongue, crisp, pulls against the dry lips and powdery roof of the mouth. Jack's skin is slick, spotted with sweat. The seat creaks when he shifts his legs. Uncomfortable, he moves farther down the row, closer to the aisle, where he can get a better look at the parade of potential victims. He will choose carefully, with one requirement in mind—he must be *homosexual*.

The video flickers, dims, and then brightens, hazy through a film of smoke. He places his right thumb on the pulse in his left wrist. Ninety-two beats per minute. Elevated, but not out of control. For a time, he ignores the sexual dance on the screen and the hover of men behind him, as time drifts like a boat on heated summer swells. He gorges on the sexual heat rising within him. His arms and legs tingle in anticipation of the deathly dance he has choreographed.

An acrid mix of smoke, disinfectant, and sex digs into his nostrils, and the smell awakens him to the screen where two men, naked and aroused, bend over a woman. The sexual abandonment goes on around him; grunts and moans of orgiastic pleasure.

A man, early twenties he guesses, eases into the seat next to him. He avoids any contact as the man eyes him, and a cold wall grows between them.

It's no surprise that a man would cruise him. Jack's been told he's handsome—a bit rough trade—but with that label he attracts a certain crowd. He can charm sex from almost anyone, like coaxing a genie from a bottle. Women want him. He's had his share. He desires them and responds to their bodies. But men want him too"—a feeling different from being wanted by a woman. An anxious rigidity tears at his body when he's with a man. It is draining for him to have sex with men, but he goes through hell for the click in the head that brings him peace. He can smell the men in the theater. He longs to touch them as blue electric waves of sexual arousal over him.

The other man, dark and thin, freezes, unsure of his next move. He looks away for a moment, shifts in his chair as if he is about to leave, but changes his mind. The young man reaches for Jack and rests his fingers on Jack's right leg. He rubs his hand up and down Jack's thigh.

Jack must be cautious, certain that this prey is what he wants. "Not now," Jack says. His gaze never leaves the screen as he pushes the man's hand away. Bundles of nerve endings fire in unison.

The young man grunts, rises from the seat, and vanishes into the murk.

Men shuffle in the aisles. Some scurry around Jack. The seats squeak three rows in front of him. He watches the bobbing heads and hears the shallow moans of ecstasy.

Ten minutes later, the dark man passes near him ready to try again.

A good sign. This man is unfazed by rejection, willing to take a risk. Jack shifts, unbuckles his belt, and pushes his jeans down to his knees.

The man stares at the naked feast before him.

Sitting, legs apart, hands molded to his thighs, Jack is a giant, but the man who kneels before him is scum. Scum services him; scum knows its place on the dirty floor. The reel of hate rolls in Jack's mind: the dirt and filth and guilt and shame. This forbidden attraction electrifies his senses—a craving so seductive he can only follow where he is led, puppet-like and numb. Long ago, he attempted to understand the prickly emotions that swamped him. But recently, like an addict, he succumbed to his cravings.

Jack offers no resistance as the man separates his legs with a gentle push from his palms. He shivers at his touch. The rough caress of his genitals shocks him into a vacant, dry world outside his body. A memory washes over him. He remembers the child he once was and despises him. He commands his mind to *shut the fuck up.*

Jack's hands tighten over the man's head and he pushes it with force into his crotch. In the flickering light, he memorizes the face, the eyes that somehow glitter when they look at him, the clothes of the man who kneels before him. Jack could kill him now—pull the knife from his jean's pocket and slash it across the neck, the jugular blood spilling frothy and dark, but the risk is too great, the scream too loud, the death struggle too violent.

Instead, he will wait until the time is right, ease through the sex and coddle intimacy for the sake of the kill.

In the alley, Jack peers over the wooden fence. The city is still, mostly asleep, but this is the house he seeks. This is the address of the man who is a threat; the man who should keep his nose out of other people's business.

Inside, two men move in front of the courtyard door. The light behind them throws soft shadows. What if they were stripped of this protection: the walls, the door, the curtains gone? What surprises Jack would have in store for *him*, the one he seeks. The other might have to be disposed of too—but he is insignificant collateral damage—a small glitch in his plan.

The lights go dark, the door swings open, and a face peers into the courtyard.

Jack ducks below the fence.

"Who's there? I know you're out there."

The voice. Jack remembers it. He crouches and then scurries like a rat down the alley. When he stops under a streetlight two blocks away, he looks at his hands, spits into them, and rubs.

Blood is plentiful when you carve like a butcher.

He must wear stronger gloves next time.

CHAPTER
TWO

STEPHEN CROSS RANG MY BUZZER AT 10 A.M. MONDAY
morning, June 26th. I ignored the first two rings because I was
sleeping with a young man I had picked up the night before
at the Manhole. The third and fourth rings seemed urgent,
and, on a persistent fifth ring, I pulled on a cream silk slip
and leather boots and headed down from my third-floor apartment. I stopped behind the green, pockmarked metal door at
the bottom of the stairs. My building was less than top-notch
South End—this was no Union Park. The gay gentry, if they
ever ventured this deep into the wasteland, would sneer at my
wretched quarters. The building's foyer was prison-like, small,
cramped, dark, and with a cement floor that clicked loudly
when traversed in heels. Any trace of the building's former
elegance had vanished—another Boston dwelling lost to neglect
in a declining neighborhood.

I peered out the small rectangular window secured by chicken
wire. I recognized Stephen Cross through the cross-hatching,
looking tired and pale. At first, I couldn't understand what he

was saying. Then I figured out he was mouthing the word *murder*. We had last seen each other six weeks ago at Café Ole, our usual meeting spot. Stephen's dark hair framed a milky face. He looked too serious, too ghostly for a beautiful June morning in Boston. I hadn't invited him over.

A fire burned in my gut, ignited by a smoldering crush. Despite my romantic fantasies for the man outside my door, I wished Stephen would leave me the fuck alone with the man upstairs. At least I had a chance with my trick. My excursion to the Manhole had been my first night out in a month.

Stephen had never set foot in my apartment. Few had. But the word *murder* intrigued me, so I opened the door and waved him in. Dressed in khaki shorts and a white T-shirt, he looked as if he had just come from the beach. The slight heft in his face betrayed his age. He *was* over forty. He *wasn't* what some girls would call handsome, but there was a gentle strength in the structure of his face, which was accented by waves of black hair and dark brows over blue eyes. Too Byronic for some. Just right for me.

I coughed.

"Smoking too much," he said in a *sotto voce* delivery.

This from a fellow cigarette sucker.

"Please, don't start. Social smoker, indeed."

Thin lines leading back from the eyes, others, deeper around the mouth, traced his face. I had to pick at him, otherwise I might place him on the pedestal of perfection. I was tempted to shove him against the wall and get nasty in the foyer.

"Who's dead?" I asked, my common sense getting the better of my fantasy.

"Like to invite me up, Des?" His voice echoed up the stairwell. "I'd prefer not to talk here, if that's okay."

As our friendship had developed, I allowed Stephen to use the shortened version of my female drag persona, Desdemona. Everyone else addressed me by my Christian name, Cody Harper.

Considering our history—what had drawn us together in the first place—what was a name between friends?

I looked at him hard and caught him blinking. His eyes were adjusting from the brilliant ocean blue sky outside to the cave-like atmosphere of my building. The morning was cool and pleasant, the happy summer tourist kind that only a Bostonian could truly appreciate.

"Your makeup's running," he had the nerve to point out.

I looked like a bad night at the local drag bar. My hair was a mess. The ultra blue eye shadow and frosty red on my lips had turned my face into Ronald McDonald on Quaaludes. What did he expect? The trick in my apartment had smeared my drag with his kisses.

"The brand shall go unnamed, but you can get it at Walgreen's." I started up the stairs. "Did you come to talk or give me a make-over?"

"You look better without makeup," Stephen said, offering an opinion that extinguished the embers in my gut.

"On some subjects, advice should be given with caution."

"I guess I don't understand it. You make a damn good looking woman. Damn good. The first time I saw you in drag I couldn't believe it. You were spectacular in a gold, shimmering evening gown. I can appreciate drag, but you look better as a man. You might want to cut the ponytail, too."

I scowled. "The cosmetics and the ponytail stay." I could tell Stephen's eyes were following my ass, taking in the slip and the black lace-up military boots. I was as sexy as any man could be in a Donna Karan undergarment. "I have to shave my chest today," I added just to get a rise. "Décolletage."

"Must be rough on the Lady Gillette."

We climbed three flights of stairs stained with coffee, soda, and God knows what else. When we got to the landing outside my apartment, I reached for a spare pack of Marlboros I always kept on the hall window sill. I pointed to a hole in the glass, chicken wired as well, and to the cobwebbed pattern of fractures.

"The times we live in," I said. "A bullet, more than a month ago. I think the assassin miscalculated, thought this window was in my apartment. The gun was fired from an angle, below and outside. Such are the hazards of my profession."

I didn't know who had fired the shot. I had a few suspicions, but nothing I could prove, and I wasn't about to go to the police. The bullet hole made for good effect, but I doubted it was fired to do me in, despite my off-and-on work as a bodyguard. It was more likely another random shooting in the city battleground. Stephen studied the powdery blotch on the ceiling.

I lit a cigarette with a flame-thrower of a Bic. "Fag? I asked.

"Later. I've been smoking too much lately."

I shrugged and opened my door. "Enter at your own risk. Just so you know, there's a man in my bed. And watch the records." To cross the room, Stephen had to walk around a few of my long-playing discs I'd tossed casually on the floor. Way too many books, Broadway cast albums, and theater posters crowded my studio apartment.

My *homme du jour* slept under the leather showcase tacked to the wall behind my bed: a collection of whips of various sorts, some ending in feather lashes, others stricter and less pliable; a cat-o-nine tails; chest harnesses with silver O-rings; leather collars with D-rings; Chaps; Jock straps; And an array of cock rings and dildos of various sizes.

Stephen gazed upon the slight young man with dark hair and smooth chest who slept in my bed. His thin wrists were secured by leather straps to the posts above his head. Danny was covered with a sheet from waist to feet, his legs splayed under the covering, his ankles tied to the bottom posts by straps as well. My trick showed an ample bulge that rose under the sheet at crotch level.

"Is he alive?" Stephen asked. "And legal?"

At times, I allowed my coarser incarnation to spring full-blown to the fray. People like Stephen brought that out in me. I got a perverse thrill not only from taking him down a notch now and then, but by pushing the boundaries of our relationship. I pursed my lips and hissed out a puff of smoke. I pulled down the sheet with a flourish and exposed the naked body under it. Danny's penis, at first asleep, pulsed into an erection.

"Look's alive to me," I said. "Of course he's legal. What kind of fool do you take me for? I picked him up last night at the Manhole. Have to show ID there. Great fuck, big dick. He snorted a little too much powder, but not enough to damage the plumbing."

Stephen didn't flinch. Or maybe he wasn't paying attention. I'd given him enough of a show, along with free admission. I pulled up the sheet and sat in the overstuffed chair that took up the corner across from my bed.

"Throw me a fag," Stephen said.

I tossed him the Marlboros.

"You doing coke again?" he asked.

I huffed in disgust. "I'm clean and you know it. Nothing's changed since that deranged queen fired the .38 at my head." Fortunately, the bullet had only traveled through the fleshy part of my left arm. Never trust a drag queen with a gun. "She's still working the streets. We exchange cordial greetings now and then, like 'Hello, motherfucker, been to target practice lately?' Honestly, I don't think she remembers shooting me."

The memory made me itchy and irritable. Suddenly, I wasn't in the mood for company. I wanted to be alone with my thoughts and my books, my silence restored. I looked at Stephen like a cat about to snag a mouse, intent and deadly. He caught my irritation.

"I came by to talk," he said in a tone as timid as I could remember. "That okay?"

His question ended in a slight drawl. At times, I could hear

Kansas all over Stephen. His years in New England had obliterated all but a trace of his dialect, usually his voice sounded as flat as a prime-time newscaster. But he would sprinkle his speech with "boys", or "damn good", or "put up", instead of put away, his unconscious journey into regionalism. At times I'd think Ma and Pa Kettle were lurking around the corner about to crank up the jalopy.

"In the two years I've known you, we've never been in each others' apartments. You can see I'm busy. What's the emergency?"

His face darkened. "There's been a murder."

I was quite certain that Stephen, the good boy political writer from Kansas, had not killed his lover, John Dresser, the handsome, wholesome pin-up boy from Vermont.

"So why come to me?" I asked. In fact, I knew the answer—our strange, symbiotic relationship with violence.

"You know who's out on the street, Des."

"Hustlers, dealers, bad boys, small-time cons, grifters, yes. Murderers, no. Who was snuffed?"

"A nice boy from Dorchester. Garbage men found him under trash bags on Providence Street—where the hustlers hang. I've been to District already to get more information. This kid wasn't out for money. Strictly middle class. No history of hustling." Stephen tilted his head back and puffed smoky O's toward the ceiling.

"People get killed all the time. What makes this one so special?"

"This one is different. The kid's throat was slashed. The murderer left a signature—a swastika carved into the thigh. And, just to make sure everyone got the point, genital mutilation."

"Nasty." I crossed my legs and my slip bristled against my thighs. "How do you know the killer's a man?"

"I don't. The cops suspect it from the crime, the strength required to make the wounds. There were signs of a struggle on

Providence Street. A lot of blood spilled. A couple of not-so-reliable regulars saw the kid in the Combat Zone around midnight at the Déjà Vu Theater. The truth is he disappeared for five hours only to turn up in the trash. The family's devastated and ashamed. They claim he wasn't gay, just lonely. Straight movies at the Déjà Vu, you know. The mayor's hell-bent, on a jag, clamoring to shut down the Zone. The usual political windfall."

He took another drag on the cigarette and stared at me. "Have you been there?"

Stephen was fishing, but I wasn't about to bite. "I haven't been to the Zone since sobriety kicked in. When I go out, I drink mineral water with lime. If I have sex, it's with someone I've known for more than three minutes—at least three hours. Very PC, you know."

Stephen tilted his head toward Danny.

"Believe me," I said, "we spent two hours in conversation. He's from Ohio, lives in Back Bay, a grad student at Emerson. He likes club music, winter camping, Joyce Carol Oates and mild, kinky sex. He scored some coke—his mistake. Besides, I was at the Manhole, not an NA meeting. I like him. I'll probably see him again. He won't be doing drugs around me."

Stephen looked away to the great altar of my room—a polished oak bookcase on the west wall. The case held my collection of American and English plays. The gold lettering on a few expensive leather bindings reflected the morning light that filtered through my windows. I knew what he was thinking: *Who would believe he reads this stuff?* It seemed there was always room for one more tragedy in my life. Some nights I fell asleep with Shakespeare and Arthur Miller on my stomach. God, what a threesome we made.

I caught the look in his eyes and said, "Everyone thinks hustlers and strippers are stupid—dealers, junkies, and pimps are morons. They may take the shaft in life, but they're not all idiots."

"I never said you were stupid, Des. If I felt that way I wouldn't have come here in the first place."

"So, I'm a little touchy. Degrees aren't everything are they? Street learning means something."

Stephen looked around the room with his reporter's eye. He would inspect and file away in his analytical and conservative brain all he considered odd about my life. I valued what little I had: my collection of cast albums, my Broadway posters from the 1970s that hung on the walls, my leather. I had haunted Shubert Alley before I left New York City. I worked as a hustler and dancer in a club around the corner. Most of the stuff I found on the street or managed to get for a quarter. If Stephen didn't like my taste, that was too bad. It was another reason for me to take him down a notch.

I returned to the bed and put my hand on Danny's left leg. He shifted, still asleep, until the straps grew taut.

A cloud passed in front of the sun and the room darkened. Stephen looked blankly into the bookcase. Then he rubbed his palms together and bowed his head. I wanted to invite him into my arms because I sensed his sadness.

His voice came out in a thin whisper. "The night you saved me...I still have nightmares."

While night's black agents to their preys do rouse.

He had come a hairsbreadth himself of being killed. I had saved his life the night he was stabbed outside a bar on Tremont Street. I tore off his bloody shirt and made a compress to stop the blood gushing from the wound over his stomach. I pushed down with blood-soaked hands and screamed for help until someone called an ambulance. That was how we met.

"This murder brings it all up again," he said. "The knife. The stabbing. I remember the heat, the emptiness. I *knew* I was going to die. I can't shake that feeling." He pulled at the leather strap which hung around his neck. At the end of the strap, concealed by his shirt, was the bullet the doctors had taken from my shoulder when Miss Deranged had tried to blow my head off. I had given the bullet to Stephen as a gift, a remembrance of our shared history with violence. He wore it every time we met, and I assumed he never took it off. I wondered what his boyfriend, John, thought when the cool metal brushed against him in bed.

"There's something else." Stephen's brow furrowed.

I looked into his eyes and saw a spit of fear.

"John and I thought we heard something in the alley last night. I stepped out and thought I saw a figure behind the fence. I checked this morning. Someone scratched a swastika into the wood. The coincidence to the Déjà Vu killing is too close for comfort. Truth be told, I'm a little scared. I want to know what's circulating on the street."

"I'll try, but I don't get out much anymore," I said. I didn't know how to offer him more comfort.

Danny snorted and his eyes fluttered. Stephen made leaving motions.

Something was missing and it bothered me. "You've covered gay bashings and murders for years. Why is this queer from Dorchester any different? Is there some connection–"

He stopped me cold with his grin, like a Halloween skull, tortured and sardonic.

"Des, would you kill me for half-a-million dollars?" he asked flatly.

Danny's eyes blinked open. He turned his head toward Stephen.

"Who the hell is he?" Danny asked in a sleepy drawl.

I clamped my hand over the kid's mouth. "Who gave you permission to speak, slave?

CHAPTER THREE

HE PARKS HIS VAN UNDER THE DARK BRANCHES OF a maple, staying away from the overhead lights, far from the rest stop's white colonial façade. He must be cautious, away from prying eyes and security cameras. He looks for cars. Men parked alone. There are a few, but too near the entrance to be possibilities.

He sits for twenty minutes in the lot, drinking a beer and punching the radio dial, until a black Chevrolet sedan passes behind him. He rolls down his window halfway and makes eye contact with the driver, a white man in his early forties. The car pulls into a parking space three down from the van.

Time drags by for another ten minutes—the 25 feet between them is a chasm—a gap guarded by anonymity, mistrust, and silence. He stares at the Chevy's driver. Their eyes meet and lock. A prickle creeps up his skin. The night air on the edge of a lush, warm softness, transforms into a crackling blue haze. He rolls up his window, locks the van, and strolls to the car.

He stops a few feet away from the window and looks into the man's face. It is kind and giving, and he is glad because kindness

—a weakness—will make the killing easier. A man who is angry is difficult because it fuels the hatred in him—an explosive situation.

The man's features are ordinary: a bit of gray in a black mustache, short hair on the balding head, wire-framed glasses bridging a thin nose. He wears a gold wedding ring on his left hand.

Jack hitches his thumb into his jean pocket and nods.

"Hi," the man says.

"Nice night."

"Yes." The man taps his fingers on the steering wheel.

"Looking for relief?"

The man looks away toward the rest stop and then back. "I know you won't believe me, but I've never done this before."

A short laugh. "Oh, a virgin to the tearoom."

The man chuckles nervously. "Yeah, to this. I've stopped here enough. I know what goes on."

A warm breeze curves around him and Jack relaxes for a moment. "Married?"

The man stares at his left hand.

"It's okay. Pussy not enough for you?"

"Look, maybe this isn't going to—"

"Come down to the van. It's private. You'll have a good time. That's why you're here, isn't it?"

The man sits, silent, staring through the windshield into the dark woods beyond.

"What's your name?" Jack coaxes. He wants him now and would do almost anything to get him to the van.

"Ron."

"Ron—I'm Jack," he says almost sweetly. He avoids a handshake or any contact with the car.

Ron grips the steering wheel and says, "I wouldn't think someone like you would be interested in someone like me."

"But I *am* interested in you. You're just my type. Guys who are married are stable. Not like your normal queer. I get off on guys who like a quiet evening at home. You know—the romantic type."

Ron looks at him and Jack can see he has him hooked. He's as good as dead.

"What the hell. That's why I'm here." He rolls up the Chevy's windows, locks the doors, and walks back to the van with Jack. Ron opens the door and hops into the passenger seat.

Jack climbs into the driver's seat, then leans across and locks the passenger door—he had already made sure the other doors were locked. He places his right hand on Ron's leg and runs his fingers up and down the slick fabric of his dress pants. He can see the stiffening bulge in Ron's crotch. Jack leans closer and in one move pulls the open cuff that's attached to the seat and clamps it onto Ron's left wrist. He moves for his gun just as fast.

"Don't move and don't say a word," Jack says. "We're going for a ride." He starts the van and pulls out of the lot while holding the gun to Ron's temple. As soon as he's on the road, he lowers the gun. "Okay, let's have some fun."

Ron is silent, shivering in his seat, but finally manages to ask, "What do you want? You want money? You can have my wallet."

Jack laughs and the power that fills him when he kills washes over him. "No, I want *you*. Just like I said. You want to get fucked don't you? Well, that's what's going to happen."

"Please...don't do this. My wife and kids will be looking for me."

"Ron. I don't want to tell you this again. Shut the fuck up." Jack slides his hand under the seat, takes out the slapjack and pops it against Ron's left temple. Ron's head lolls and then he slumps forward against the dashboard, the cuff cutting into his wrist.

* * *

Ron wakes from a hazy dream, his head throbbing—like he was underwater, but a dim light filters into his eyes. The air is humid in the back of the van, with a scent of pine, sweat, and the acidic bite of fear. He shakes his head and the fuzz clears a little. He tries to move; the maneuver is useless. His legs and wrists are bound to O rings secured to the van's bed. He is naked, stomach down on the floor. He whispers a brief, hoarse call for help. No one answers and the silence stings him.

A few minutes later, the van's rear doors open and Ron strains to look over his shoulder. Gloved hands slide over his buttocks. "Do you like it, Ron? That's what you want, don't you? You want to get fucked."

"Stop. I'll give you whatever you want—you can have it."

"I don't want anything."

The gloves move up the cleft of his back, toward his shoulders and stop on his neck. They linger too long and Ron shakes them away, but the grip tightens.

"Why would you want to do that? Don't you want your lover's touch?"

The hands squeeze and Ron gasps for air, his lungs burning for breath. Then, as quickly as they closed around his windpipe, they open, and he gasps down the sticky air.

Jack's voice is soft, mockingly erotic. "You want it, don't you pervert? Faggot. If you want to get fucked—fuck this." Jack leans over him. The gloved hands are replaced by something that feels like a cool metal rod. It doesn't take long for Ron to realize that Jack is scraping a gun barrel across his back.

The barrel slides down to the cleft of his buttocks and the cold steel runs up and down like a metal finger between his testicles and rectum. He stifles a scream as the gun pushes against his perineum and then lifts to his anus.

Jack takes excited short breaths.

The barrel cuts into Ron's rectum, the pistol sight rips the tissue as it jabs his insides.

Ron screams and Jack slams Ron's head against the van floor. Again. And again.

When he comes to, he is face down on the damp earth, gasping for breath. A fiery pain travels from his head to his toes. His right jaw is shattered. His glasses are gone and one eye is covered by a bloody red film; through the other he sees the dark outline of legs to his right. A booted foot pushes down on the back of his head, crushing his face into the ground. The rocky earth muffles his screams. His bound hands struggle to catch the grip of the gun still inside him.

Strong hands part his legs.

The voice is soothing, gentle. "Thanks, Ron, for the one-night stand."

The gloved hand pushes against his buttocks.

The gun fires. The bullet rips through him and his world plunges into darkness.

* * *

New Hampshire State Trooper William Anderson is the first officer to arrive at 9:32 p.m. on July 3rd off Route 119 near Fitzwilliam. He opens the patrol car door and tosses his nearly finished cigarette on the ground. He crushes the butt with his boot and pulls on his jacket. The day, warm and muggy this holiday weekend, has faded and the night brings relief from the heat. The temperature, about 72, is dropping and the wind sharpens off the peaks. *Rain would be nice*, he thinks. The ground is dry and cracked. So much can go wrong on the Fourth. Rain would keep people indoors, maybe fewer drunk drivers, boating accidents, drownings and hiking mishaps. *Protect and serve, my ass. More like babysit and clean up the mess.*

He radios headquarters he is on site and soon to be out of the car. He checks his right jacket pocket for a pad and pen and then lifts the portable light from the seat. He switches on the vehicle's rotating beacons and the lights vibrate violently against the black pines before being sucked into the darkness.

About fifty yards to his left, on a dirt construction access road, flashlight beams scatter through banks of bushy undergrowth and reflect off the white birches.

"Over here," a man yells. Other voices break into chatter.

Trooper Anderson focuses the beam in front of him and pushes through the trees in a zig-zag walk past low, leafy branches.

He mentally prepares himself for the body. No matter how many times he's seen a victim, no matter how hard he tries, he never quite gets over knowing that the flesh in front of him was once a living, breathing human. Some scenes are worse than others. Kids, particularly, or those that look like slaughterhouse leftovers.

Dust motes whirl through the scattered light. Smoke wafts from the red tips of cigarettes. Three men from a construction company in Nashua huddle in a cramped circle over a dark form on the ground. They break from the circle and back away. Their lights careen down.

"Jesus, God," the trooper says.

"I came over to take a leak," a stocky young man says. "Just finished cutting a road through the lots. Thought I saw a leg."

The body, festering, bloated, is face down on the forest floor.

Anderson gawks at the corpse. "I've never seen...."

"We've been prepping all day," another man says and flicks an ash from his cigarette. "Owner wants to get the house up by winter."

Anderson tracks his light down the body from head to toe. The blast has blown away part of the lower back and buttocks. Blackened blood coats the back and shoulders; a dried inky stream runs from the waist.

"He's got something God-awful clutched in his left hand," the second man says.

Anderson kneels for a closer look. He studies the top of the discolored hand, the distended fingers, which he can imagine before death as fair-skinned and fine with little hair. An etched gold band cuts into the fourth left finger which is the greenish color of bad meat. He plays the light into the tight circle of fingers and peers into the fist.

The trooper's stomach turns a little. "It's a dick," Anderson says.

FOUR

THE PHONE RANG SATURDAY MORNING AND I
ignored it.

I cinched my leather harness and assumed the role of master.
Danny responded, his erection growing underneath the sheet. I
instructed him not to move—to keep his eyes on the ceiling – and
selected a feather whip and alligator teeth tit clamps for play.

Danny moaned lightly under the whip. His nipples rose into
purple buds when I attached the clamps. I placed my left hand over
his mouth and commanded him to lick it clean, finger by finger.
He took my thumb into his mouth and sucked. I lashed his groin
and the inside of his thighs as he washed my fingers. As the master,
I maintained the precise measure of the whip: enough force to
sting the skin with pleasure, but not enough to cause harm. Under
the lash, Danny bent like a sapling. After he had completed the
service on my hand, I took one of his socks and stuffed it into his
mouth. Then, I lit a candle and dripped hot wax from his sternum
to groin. His body shivered with each white drop.

The phone rang for a second time—ten annoying rings.

I freed Danny's hand and allowed him to masturbate to orgasm. I released his bindings and we showered together. I permitted Danny to wash and kiss me, and then I washed and kissed him.

When the phone rang the third time, Danny shot me an exasperated look, chiding me for being such a Luddite.

"I am not getting an answering machine," I said.

We sat naked on the bed and talked for an hour. Then, while he kissed me, Danny eased into his clothes. I was ready for round two, but my less-than-subservient slave had plans for the afternoon. We promised to get together for a movie in a couple of days. He kissed me and then left. I pulled the weights from under my bed and worked out for 45 minutes. Then, I put on a light cotton robe and stretched out across the bed. The room was dim under a low, gray July sky.

A couple of years ago, I visited a fortune teller who had a little business on the edge of Bay Village. A garish storefront window, with a blinking red neon sign and curtains of brightly colored beads strung across it, called to any suckers who passed by. There was a green door with an outstretched yellow hand, palm forward, painted on the glass. I was always on the fence about such hocus-pocus, not really believing in palmistry, séances, or other such nonsense, but, on a whim, I decided to give this woman a try. Perhaps I had puffed too much grass that day. I opened the door and the tangy smell of paprika entered my nose. She lived upstairs and had a pot of goulash on the stove. The munchies kicked in as she descended the stairs. She was a short European woman with curly black hair and legs as thick as tree trunks.

"You half the geeft of proph-ee-see," she said in her best fake gypsy accent. That's about all I remember from an hour long session which emptied my wallet of $100. But I never forgot her pronouncement.

Too bad I had lacked the gift to foretell Stephen's attack, when the knife missed his stomach and liver by centimeters. The assailant was a kid—at least that was the word on the street – a hatemonger, a dangerous boy playing with a sharp toy. The fool should have known better than to stab a gay newspaper columnist and ex-police reporter. All the rags raged, including the straight press, but no knife was ever found, no arrests ever made.

My supposed gift was even worse when it came to Ms. Deranged. I was shot in the left arm when I made a stupid attempt to skim money from a triple threat—drag queen, crack cocaine dealer, and pimp. Needless to say, she was pissed. I reported to the unforgiving and unimpressed police that I was shot in an attempted robbery. Stephen, being my best buddy after saving his life, made pilgrimages to my cheerfully drab hospital room for a couple of days. After my recovery, I gave him the bullet and went cold turkey on all sauces: herbal, capsule, powder, and liquid. Stephen's boyfriend John stepped back, allowing our time together, realizing we had formed our own strange bond.

Since Stephen's visit to inform me about the Combat Zone killing, I had been incessantly plagued by my dreams of death and cold. A particularly disturbing one involved a naked man strapped to a wooden slab in a Nazi laboratory. He was being tortured by a sadistic young soldier. So, in my dreams and even awake, I started to see—picture—this soldier, the man who killed. The resolution was fuzzy, the face indistinct, but I knew he was real even though he was a product of my dreams. That much I surmised. But there was much more I couldn't put my finger on. In my waking hours, the soldier was never in the Zone, but far away in a cluttered room with little light and close air—a horror of a space—but full of the possibility of answers, like a Ouija Board gone bad.

* * *

I was sleeping, curled into a tight ball, clammy from the dream. In some odd way, whatever the mind dreams, the mind knows. Dreaming is wonderful if there are no nightmares. But who has such a luxury? I pulled the blanket over me and prayed to be saved by an absent God. Nothing is as damning as the silence in your head after a prayer.

The phone rang. This time I answered.

Wonder of wonders, Stephen Cross was on the line. His voice had that edgy, anxious tone of a father who's lost his child in a department store.

"I was with Danny—as if it's any of your business," I said, making my excuse for not answering the phone earlier.

"Get a goddamn machine," Stephen replied tartly.

"Out of the question. One, I don't like them. Two, I don't have the money for such extravagances."

"A machine is not an extravagance, it's a necessity. We're ready to enter the 21st Century, yet no one can reach you. Hermits are very passé."

"That's the way I like it," I said, growing annoyed at Stephen's jabs.

"No wonder you don't make enough money for extravagances. If you don't answer the phone, no one can hire you for your services."

My irritation faded. "Okay, point taken," I said. "You need a bodyguard?"

"Yeah, just in case." He relaxed a little and the tension began to melt.

"You want to talk?"

"I'd rather you come by for conversation—let's say a verbal three-way in about an hour."

"I didn't think you and John were into that."

"We're not. John's at work. I've got a call into District Four.

Chris Spinetti will be by." Stephen's voice sparkled a little.

The hair on the back of my neck bristled. I had no use for Spinetti, a Boston police detective. I could barely hide my disgust for the dick. After I was shot, Chris had driven me to hell and back and since then had almost singlehandedly ruined my career. I was annoyed by Stephen's tempered glee.

"I couldn't care less about seeing Chris, and I'm sure he feels the same way."

"Get over it," Stephen said. "I want you to know everything. You're my pipeline, Des, and my bodyguard."

Was that all Stephen saw in me—security? What about John, the boy wonder? How was he at protection? I had never offered my heart to Stephen; after all, I really wasn't the marrying kind, but I sent out signals he couldn't ignore. Little looks I shot his way during our monthly get-togethers. For the first time in my life, I had sampled what it might be like to be in love, and I liked it. But, as any grade school student knows, there has to be a sender and a receiver for two-way communication, and no messages had been received, no hints taken.

There was an uncomfortable silence before I responded with a simple, "Thanks."

"There's been another murder," Stephen said, his voice edgy again.

I was silent.

"In New Hampshire," he continued, "but it matches the pattern of the Combat Zone killing. A married man, for Christ's sake. He took his last cruise at the rest stop on I-93 in Salem. His cock ended up in his left hand." He stifled a half-hearted chuckle. "Not attached. When they turned the body over they found a swastika carved into his thigh." Stephen sighed. "Remember Edward the Second?"

I wanted to say something flip like, "*Not, personally, but if you're speaking of Marlowe's play...*," but I couldn't. All I could imagine was that bloody body on the ground. Instead I said, "King of England, 1307 to 1327, the son of Edward the First and Eleanor of Castille. The first Prince of Wales—"

"—Sorry, should have known better. This man died like Edward, but instead of Isabella and Mortimer ordering the death of the King by the insertion of a red-hot poker in the rectum, this killer updated his modus operandi for the '90s. A .357 up the ass."

The soldier from my dream popped back into my head.

"I was in a bookstore looking for Shakespeare's plays. *Macbeth* or *Julius Caesar*. The ceiling was vaulted and through the window I saw a flying buttress. Then the dream shifted in an instant, the way dreams do, and I was standing in the snow outside a small wooden hut."

"What the hell are you talking about?" Stephen asked.

"This afternoon...when I was sleeping. I opened the door to the hut, wanting to get out of the cold, and I saw a naked man on a tilted wooden slab. He was barely alive, his face drawn and ashen, and colored with streaks of sea-foam green. His right arm was stripped free of skin from shoulder to elbow, muscle and tendon exposed. The soldier who was torturing him drew his pistol and fired. He shouted something when he pulled the trigger."

"*Arschficker?*" Stephen asked.

"It could have been. I don't know German. But there was something even more disturbing—in the corner was a metal vat filled with freezing water, it smelled of salt and frost. There was a man surrounded by chunks of ice, his skin was shimmering, blue with cold. I couldn't understand what he was shouting, but he kept calling to me, arms outstretched. He wanted me to save him and I couldn't.... And then the soldier killed him, too."

I could feel the goose bumps run over Stephen's body. It took him a few seconds to compose himself before he said, "Sometimes you scare me, Des. Don't tell me any more dreams. Please come over."

"Dangerous stuff is going down," I said. "I know it from the dream."

I hung up after promising to be over in an hour. I took off my robe, dropped it on the bed and walked to the shower. Little beads of sweat ran down my neck and chest, and I was strangely cold for a warm July afternoon, but the hot water soon warmed my body and soul. As I relaxed in the steam, I made up my mind to keep select details of my personal life from Stephen Cross. After all, in my dream he was the man in the vat.

The trip to Stephen's was an excuse to get out of my apartment, shake off my lethargy, and rejuvenate my dislike for Chris Spinetti. The murders, my sense of mortality, hammered a cat-like arch of anxiety into my back. No matter how tenuous the thread, there was a connection between Stephen and me (as John had recognized). Usually, the shared violence of our histories guided our conversations, but when we were together we sometimes talked about his writings, the theories he advanced, the groups he discussed in his weekly column. We talked about Democrats, Republicans, Liberals, Conservatives, Protestants, Catholics, the Christian Right, the militia movement, neo-Nazis, and gay bashers. We rarely talked about sex. Of all these topics, Stephen was most interested in Nazis and gay bashers, whom he saw as an increasing threat inspired by the politics of the country. I wasn't quite sure of the reasons for his fascination with things National Socialist, but I suspected it had to do with his struggle to understand such movements, combined with the lingering effects of the violence he had experienced.

While pondering my relationship with Stephen, I also wondered what I might do to annoy my old friend Chris Spinetti. If he was the closet case I suspected, nothing would set him off like a good dose of drag. I pulled a white cotton slip with lace trim from my dresser, slipped it on, and tucked it into a pair of black jeans. I had mastered that maneuver long ago with some artful diapering of the crotch. I chose a leather jacket and a pair of boots to complete my outfit. The afternoon air was misty and cool enough for heavier clothing.

Stephen and John lived at 308 Channing, west of my apartment on the same street. The fifteen-minute walk took me past the Victorian brownstones of the South End—the graceful, curving bow fronts constructed 120 years ago that lined the street like the crests of waves. My end of Channing was dirtier and dingier: the red bricks had turned a sad brown. Stephen and John were strictly upper class compared to my neighborhood. The classy end of Channing had no burned-out buildings, no drug dealers smoking crack on the stoop, no homeless living under the steps. Three-zero-eight was in a "better part" of the South End with clean-swept gutters, gas lamps that worked, and pruned maple and ash trees protected by ornamental wrought-iron guards.

At 2:30 p.m., I walked up the high concrete steps to Stephen's apartment and rang the buzzer, about a half-hour before Chris was scheduled to arrive. Stephen, wearing only a blue towel wrapped around his waist, peered through the double-glass doors. Unlike his lover, John, Stephen was displaying the slight paunch common to most over-forty American males. And, horror of horrors, I spotted patches of white scalp through the strands of his wet black hair. I lowered my gaze to steal a peak at his towel-covered crotch. Nothing extraordinary there. I mentally slapped myself for being such a bitch and then chalked it up to jealousy. I admired the man and his life more than I cared to admit. If only our lives had not been so different, I could have taken my "crush" to a whole different level. I envied Stephen and John, in their home, safe and comfortable in their monogamous relationship. They were real. They meant something.

"You're early," he said, sounding eerily similar to Michael in *The Boys in the Band*, except the line to Harold was "*You're late.*"

"I just got out of the shower," he said, drily.

"No kidding."

He ushered me through a tasteful hall decorated with expensive table lamps and landscape prints and into the apartment. The living room with its wood-burning fireplace, large bay window, and chintz settee seemed as composed and cheerful as a Mozart piano concerto. Stephen told me to make myself at home and then left the room.

I thought I might help myself to the scotch on the drinks tray, but sobriety got the better of me. I snooped around. The apartment looked "cozy and nice". That's how anyone's maiden aunt would have described it. There were two side chairs at each end of the settee. Dark walnut stereo speakers nestled in the curve of the window. There was no shortage of *objet d'art* on the fireplace mantle: a clock, silver candlesticks, bronze reproductions of Chinese horses, wooden curio boxes—all very South End cachet.

The dining room, connected to the living room by a pair of French doors, was less ornate. A round oak table skirted by four chairs filled the room. A laptop computer sat on a rolling cart in the corner. Birch logs filled the room's fireplace, this one seemingly dormant all year. To the left, a small white kitchen adjoined the dining room. Stephen had disappeared down a spiral wooden staircase to a lower floor, which, I surmised, contained at least a bathroom and bedroom.

A thud echoed up the stairwell. Stephen, dressed in a white T-shirt and khaki pants, reappeared ass first in the kitchen. He grunted and tugged at a hefty wooden trunk which scraped along the tiles. He lifted the trunk and carried it to the dining room table. Flecks of red paint fell from the leather straps. Stephen withdrew a metal key from his pocket and inserted it into the lock. The lid opened smoothly. I smelled mothballs.

"I wanted to show you this," Stephen said. "It's my dad's collection from World War II. He gave it to me. I played with this stuff when I was a kid."

He lifted a steel helmet from the trunk. I recognized it as the formidable German headgear from war movies. "Waffen, SS," he explained. "The military branch of the Shutzstaffel, the protection squad formed by Himmler. The helmet has the S-rune decals of the SS – symbolizing the sun's life-giving powers." He handed it to me. The steel was cool to the touch.

Stephen reached into the trunk and pulled out a long, gray coat with black epaulets.

"My father took this from a dead SS Captain in December 1944."

"Charming," I said, wondering if this display had reached its peak of morbidity.

"He smuggled this stuff out," Stephen continued. "He would tell me stories about the war and I would dream of fighting in France, trudging from village to village, hunkering down in a snowy foxhole with my rifle, and then, after the fighting was over, drinking wine in front of a fireplace in the home of a grateful French partisan." He laughed. "War was romantic when I was a kid. I have hobnail boots and a visor field cap as well." He lifted a small gray hat from the trunk. The empty eyes of a grinning skull, woven in silver thread, stared out from the cap. The skull rested below a spread-winged eagle perched on a swastika. "The skull and crossbones worn by all the SS. The Nazis gave the SS rings, as well. The death head was on the outside, and Himmler's signature inside the band. Take a look in the trunk."

Photos and letters were piled on top of books and clothing. The photos interested me. On a summer day more than fifty years ago, a German woman with short dark hair had helped her young son walk across a thick lawn. She clutched his chubby hands above his head as he teetered on his feet. Another picture was more severe: It showed the stern face of a German soldier, in dress uniform, his dark hair slicked back from his temples. His nose was long and narrow and ended in a graceful curve above his thin lips. His dark eyes stunned me with their messianic gaze. In another photo, the family dined at an outdoor picnic table near a rose trellis. A rough pencil inscription on the back read, "*Mein Herz.*"

"Most of this stuff was from this unidentified family," Stephen explained. He stared into the trunk with a kind of reverence, as if it held some mystical powers. "As a child, there was one piece I could never touch." He lifted a long bundle wrapped in a torn white sheet, placed it on the table, and unrolled it in slow turns. Eventually, the form was revealed: a gleaming steel dagger, its handle a black hourglass crowned and divided from the hilt by burnished metal. S-runes and an eagle decorated the weapon, which seemed to draw forth the powers of the Norse gods in its design. It looked expertly proportioned for killing. The six-inch blade carried the inscription, "*Meine Ehre Heisst Treue.*" I asked Stephen for a translation, although I had a good idea.

"My honor is loyalty," he said. "It's a ceremonial dagger, given to the SS men as a reward for exceptional service and merit."

I stared at the gleaming blade and got the uneasy feeling that I had met, through the photographs, the dead soldier who carried this dagger.

"The spoils of Nazi Germany. Swastikas carved into gay men. What other pleasant surprises do you have for me?"

I withdrew a cigarette from the pack I had tucked into my jeans and put it into my mouth, savoring the earthy smell of tobacco. I wondered whether I would be permitted to smoke in the *house of the clean.* He motioned for me to have a seat in the living room; I sat in one of the uncomfortable side chairs. Stephen reclined on the settee. I enjoyed the moment, my romantic notions getting the better of me. He was slightly flushed from the shower, or maybe from dragging the trunk up the stairs, but he looked comfortable and relaxed as the gray afternoon light and the brilliant green of the trees mixed in the bay window behind him. What would it be like to sit with your lover on a Sunday afternoon, have a smoke or a drink, and talk about life? The little stuff, *"How was your day, dear? What are we having for dinner tonight, sugar cakes?"* Could I really be happy in such a domestic prison? For a moment, I thought I could, as I took in Stephen's form. There was something sexy and masculine about him despite all my attempts to knock him down. I loved his studious, good looks. I wanted to run my hands over the crotch of his khakis. I removed the cigarette from my mouth and relegated it to my fingers where I could twirl it enough to annoy him.

Stephen broke my fantasy soon enough. His mouth turned down at the corners and the lines around his eyes set in deep furrows.

"John doesn't even know what I'm about to tell you," he said.

I was not flattered. "Why not? You two might as well be married," I said, trying hard to tone down my jealousy. "He's your partner—he needs to know."

"I'll tell him soon enough, but frankly Des, I didn't want him to be alarmed. He doesn't understand these things—the political machinations that drive the world. John's more concerned with biceps and triceps and the latest health food. It works for him, and that's fine. In a way, it's fine for me too. His profession keeps me grounded."

"Well then, everything's perfect here at 308."

"Hardly. When Chris gets here, he'll understand. He'll take this seriously."

I cringed at Spinetti's name. Stephen shot me a look as if I had thrown cold water in his face.

"I've had a few nasty phone calls in my career," Stephen continued, "but nothing that's bothered me this much. I've dealt with crackpots and weirdoes. I didn't worry about this at first either, but that's all changed."

He stopped and watched as I rocked the cigarette between my fingers.

"Throw me a fag," he said. "I need one."

"Mind if I join you?"

"Not at all."

"What will John say?" I threw the pack to him.

He chuckled and replied, "I'll tell him *you* wanted a smoke. Pull that Chinese dish off the mantle. It'll work as an ashtray. It's a fake anyway."

I did as instructed, put the dish on the coffee table, and settled back in my chair. I lit up and tossed my lighter to Stephen. He did the same and drew in a deep, smoky breath, which he exhaled with a grateful smile.

He ruffled his damp hair with his left hand and said, "About three months ago, on a Sunday morning, as John and I were watching television, flipping through all the crap on cable, John stopped for a moment on a religious program and I saw *the face*. This thin white face jabbering about religion—another man joined in—two men spouting talk-show generalities about Christianity. The first face knocked me right off the couch. I know this man, I thought. Praise the Lord, I know this man.

"We didn't go searching for this program. I'm a Methodist and John's a lapsed Catholic. I asked John to go back to the channel. I made up a story about watching it—that these two guys were talking about a topic I might be interested in writing about. I really wanted to make sure I wasn't losing my mind. John was disgusted by the program and walked to the kitchen to have a bit more breakfast. I was happy he left me alone.

"The channel is called 'God's Network'. I turned up the volume and listened to the voice. The man was saying, 'We need your support. Your tax-deductible contributions go to our work.

The Council for Religious Advancement remains a beacon for America...we can stop the tide of destruction from swamping America's families...we can stop the *homosexuals* and their agenda.' The usual stuff.

"When he said the word 'homosexuals', I knew. The voice, the sound of the word, the slight lilt of the Southern accent. I walked to the television and crouched down to get a better look. He was handsome in a charismatic, elegant way—older, of course, but his hair was still blond. The most beautiful mouth, gently bowed arches for lips. But it was the way he said the word—lightly, almost sweetly—that made me remember. Then he started quoting Bible verses, all the old war horses against homosexuality."

"Who is he?" I asked.

"Rodney Jessup."

"So, who's he? The only TV in my apartment is me."

"You know the Combat Zone like the back of your hand, but you don't know squat about politics. But I understand. Who knew Jim Bakker before the scandal? The Reverend Rodney Jessup recently resigned as the head of the Beacon of God Churches to run for President. When did I meet him? 1977? 1978? It was on Eighth Avenue. Your old haunt."

"I worked that street on my back."

Stephen laughed and stubbed out the cigarette he had barely smoked. "I was working for a small newspaper near New Haven, newly out, discovering my way in the world. I had this tiny apartment that overlooked the waterfront. It smelled like oil and dead fish mostly. New York City was indeed the Great White Way. It gave me hope that my life might be more than reporting about traffic light installations on Main Street. Of course, I was lonely too."

"I can hardly imagine you being lonely," I said, and hoped Stephen didn't take my comment as sarcasm.

"Oh, yes, plenty lonely. A kid from Kansas on the East Coast.

One night, I went into the city. I walked past the Hercules Theater on 49th Street. It was December, cold and windy, and the thought of heading back to my bare Connecticut apartment depressed me. So, I dug into my pocket and found five dollars—a steep but necessary price to pay for company. According to the black plastic letters plastered on the blazing white marquee, I was about to enjoy *Beach Boy Bums* and *Hot and Wild,* a decidedly entertaining double feature. I remember thinking I was ashamed of what my life had become: quick sexual encounters in a dingy porn theater."

"It's a living," I said.

"Maybe for some, but I hoped there was more to being gay than this. However, I was unsure what it was." He took another cigarette from my pack and lit up. "I was scared shitless. Every time I went to a theater I was terrified somebody would rob me or cut me up."

"Clearly an amateur, unsure of his environment."

Stephen smirked. "Yes, but sex won out on most occasions. After I paid my admission, I walked into the tacky blue lobby with beefcake photos of nude men on the walls. The place smelled like a bad mix of raw sex and disinfectant. At the end of the lobby there was a double set of stairs to the left and to the right going up to the balcony. I opened the red double doors leading into the theater, and all I saw was a smoky pall drifting across a blazing white screen. I had walked in between movies. I decided to settle in upstairs, which for some reason always seemed more inviting to me. That's when I saw him standing in the bend in the stairs. He was a tall attractive man in a tweed sports jacket. We cruised each other. He followed me into the bathroom. We barely spoke. I touched his shoulder and then he touched mine."

Stephen sighed.

"Go on," I said.

"I wanted to make sure it was all right with him. He acted as

35

if it hurt to touch me. Then, he apologized to me and said it was his first time. I wasn't sure whether to believe him, but it didn't matter. Nothing mattered in the Hercules. We sat in a deserted corner of the theater. We got together over the next three months. It was the only place he said we could meet.

"He never wanted to tell me his name, he said it didn't matter, but he said Stephen Cross was an easy name to remember. Of course, I didn't know then he might be a minister. One of the last times I saw him, we were kissing in a corner, I was rubbing my hands all over his body. After he left—because we never walked out together—I saw a white business card on the floor. Apparently, it had fallen out of one of his pockets. It's filed away somewhere—"

The phone interrupted us. I looked at the mantle clock: it was 3:15 p.m.

I heard Stephen making excuses, apologies. When he returned his face was strained, tighter.

"Spinetti can't make it. He's busy working the case in the Zone. Shit, I needed to talk to him."

"You still can," I said. "Can you get away from John for a few hours tonight? I know where we can find Chris."

I knew exactly where to find the detective. The Déjà Vu.

CHAPTER FIVE

HE SITS IN A CABIN DEEP IN THE FOREST. THE LATE afternoon sun casts long shadows of green and black. He spreads the magazines in front of him and runs his fingers over the pictures, stopping on the erect penis or the anus. He chuckles as he lifts the scissors and plunges them into the genitals. Porn magazines filled with pictures of nude men, the sexual organs torn or clipped out. He picks up a marker and blacks out the faces.

A start on the collection. He pulls a copy of *The Boston Alternative* out of a green garbage bag and leafs through the pages. He stops on a story published in May about two gay men tortured and murdered in Texas. He scrawls the words 'DESERVE IT' in black letters above the story. But he's looking for a name and he finds it on a column titled *Commonwealth Politics*. The name is Stephen Cross. He circles it and marks the byline in all the other papers he has collected. Ten in all. He smirks at the picture of the smart-ass journalist who has the balls to defend his perverted lifestyle and to criticize those who challenge it. Stephen Cross is the man he wants.

He finds a fresh sheet of paper and draws in ink the smiling face of Hitler. Underneath, he pens a swastika, drawn expertly in three-dimensional view. He turns the sheet like a wheel and in crabbed script forces the pen hard down on the paper. The name Stephen Cross flows around the edge like a sacred illuminated manuscript.

Jack. Jack the Ripper. Jack Sprat could eat no fat, his wife could eat no lean.

Jack, the little boy who lives inside him, full of tears. The house he hates and remembers.

His father whipped the puppy until it yelped in pain. He stood, tears streaming from his face, and shook, wondering if he might collapse.

"You're next, you little shit," his father said. "This dog craps in the house again, it's dead."

"Please don't hurt her."

The belt came down hard again on the soft furry back. The pup howled and wriggled its head away from his father, who held it by the scruff of the neck. The dog squirmed, dropped to the floor, and stumbled away, yowling.

"Get out of here, fucking mutt." His father kicked blindly at the dog.

"Please, daddy, don't."

"Come here, sissy. I'll teach you."

His father loomed over him, a small shivering boy. The man undid his son's pants, grabbed him by the neck, and bent him over his knee.

The belt bit into his legs and buttocks until he felt nothing. "You can join that worthless dog," his father said after the beating was through.

The puppy was shivering at the door, waiting to go outside. The boy scooped up the dog and stepped into the frigid February air. The sun was setting like a pink ball, streaking the thin winter clouds with orange and red. He was only wearing a sweatshirt and jeans, but he didn't care. He fought back tears and held the puppy close to his chest. The chubby warm bundle cried briefly and then snuggled against him as their breath puffed into steam.

"I hate you," he said to the sky. "I hate you." Then he cried over the puppy and swore he would never let his father hurt her again.

That evening, as his father sat watching television, drinking a beer and snickering at a family comedy, the boy traded his innocence for the hatred of a man. Any love he held for his father died.

CHAPTER SIX

"WHAT IS IT WITH YOU AND CHRIS?" I ASKED STEPHEN.
"I like him."

"After what he did to me?"

"He was doing his job—shaking you out. He's a cop, Des."

"He's a snake." Stephen tried to ignore my comment by staring out the bay window. I cleared my throat and he turned his attention back to me.

"Look, he's the best detective I know. Ten years on the beat—it's a hard life. He played the game, took the exam. I admire him. I know cops—I've been around them for years. When you work with them you know what they are, little boys in a man's body. They like to play cops and robbers." Stephen looked admiringly at my smokes again.

"Enough," I said, and grabbed the pack from him. "You don't pay me enough to keep me in cigarettes. Back to Chris."

"The gay rumors are bullshit," Stephen continued. "So what if he's queer? We all have our personal reasons and timeline for coming out. He's smart enough to keep his private life separated from his professional life. You'll never see Chris at a gay bar. It's bad form, socializing, picking up a guy there. The fantasy of power sex with a real cop is too inviting for most men."

"Never thought of it."

Stephen laughed, shook his head, and then said, "Yeah, right. Ninty-nine percent of gay men are willing to be ordered into handcuffs by a handsome cop who looks great in uniform. I'm sure you're among them."

"Maybe a couple of cops I know, but I never had a hankering to be bound by Chris. He wants my ass in jail."

"You had a run in with him. That's all."

"Run in? After I got shot, he nearly killed me with his endless inquisition. It was worse than the bullet. Since then, he's blocked every effort I've made to start a career as a professional body-guard, including bonding. I've been reduced to working odd jobs and catch-as-catch-can security assignments. I'm clean and I want to work. Chris doesn't seem to understand that."

I'd had enough of the uncomfortable chair and got up. "Meet me at the Déjà Vu tonight at nine. Place should be hopping on a Saturday night. Chris *will* be there."

"What makes you so sure?"

"Well, he'll say he's working overtime conducting his investigation into the murders. But my connections tell me he's there for more than work. That's the kind of information you want. That's why you came to me in the first place, isn't it?" Stephen nodded and I stopped on my way to the door. "I bet Chris buys *Playboy* to read the stories."

"I've never been to the Déjà Vu, and I'm not going alone," Stephen said. "John and I met just after I moved to Boston. The thought of going to a porn theater never entered my mind."

I wanted to say, "Unlike New York," but held my tongue. Why would he go to the Combat Zone when he could make love to John the muscle god every night? But even Adonis must get

41

boring after ten years. "You need a nasty little devil like me to show you the city's secrets. It's been really interesting cataloging Nazi memorabilia, but I've got a few things to do before I hit the streets tonight."

"John will be home in two hours," Stephen said somewhat dreamily.

"Have a nice dinner. Talk. Then tell him you're going out with your old friend Des to a porn theater."

Stephen frowned and stiffened a bit on the settee. It was my last glimpse of him before I closed the door.

I bought a newspaper at a corner store on Columbus Avenue. Danny came to mind and I remembered I wanted to pick up an item at Matt's Leather Emporium, a shop off Berkeley Street. I walked north, puffed on a cigarette, and savored the damp day, a refreshing change from the heat.

As I walked, I marveled at how Stephen trusted Chris Spinetti, considering how the detective had the opposite effect on me. A few months before, at Café Ole, Stephen had opened up about him. He had met Chris at District Four six months or so before my run in with Madame Shootatzka. Stephen was part of the Gay Pride Planning Committee (how wholesome) and he was at the station discussing traffic patterns for the annual parade. Chris was a reluctant participant from the District and had to endure the meeting while another officer, the liaison from the police department to the gay community, and Stephen went over regulations. Stephen caught Chris staring at him and the looks made him uncomfortable. During a break, Chris introduced himself and the subject drifted to Stephen's family life, and, of course, John, The Body Club, and working out—a testosterone-laced topic of male interest. Chris said Stephen could use a few rounds with the weights and *he* could give him some pointers. Never one to pass up a source, Stephen continued to call on

Chris as an informant for his journalistic endeavors. Apparently, those meetings and confidences were what held the two men together.

"The balls," Stephen had told me over coffee when recounting his first encounter with the detective. "At first, I thought he was a jerk. So, I'm a little overweight. I don't have a perfect, sculpted body, but I still have my hair, and everybody thinks I'm five years younger than I am."

"You *are* perfect," I said with the slightest hint of sarcasm.

"I know he was looking at me," Stephen said.

I smiled. "Well, I'll give Spinetti credit. He knows a good looking man when he sees one." That comment brought the conversation to a halt with a warm smile from my tablemate. So, vanity thy name *is* Stephen Cross. Maybe Stephen stroked the crotch rocket for Chris, and that was as far as Stephen was willing to go, but I was skeptical of any mutual affection from the cop. Sexual attraction is the most dangerous reason to trust anyone. That was my revelation for the day, courtesy of Stephen and two cups of coffee at Café Ole.

By the time I reached the leather shop, a light rain had begun to fall. The water glistened on the brick sidewalk and dripped from the maple leaves.

A man dressed in lace-up military boots, black jeans, and a white T-shirt stood near Matt's door. A worn leather jacket was hitched over his shoulder. He was sexy, and looked as rough trade as any man I had ever seen in the South End. My hustler eye captured him perfectly: tall, long arms and legs, the bones showed under the tight skin of his face, as if he'd had to skimp on meals. The brownish hair on his head was shaved to a stubble. But it was his eyes—two blue coal furnaces – that forced me to look away or fall into heaven by way of hell.

"Got a light?" the man asked.

I was all too happy to take my Bic out of my pants and light his cigarette. He was pretty, but I didn't want to waste time. I had come to look for ball stretchers. I reached for the door, but he stopped my arm.

"You got money? I'm no queer. I don't get fucked."

I stepped away from the door and fixed on his blues. "Just what *do* you do?"

His eyes flared for a second and then dimmed.

"I got a girlfriend. A good one." His jaw was so tight I wondered how he could talk. He tapped his boot against the sidewalk. "I don't like queers, but they pay good for me. Gets us by."

"How much?"

"Fifty."

"Look, buddy, you got the wrong number." I started to push past him, but he flung his arm across the door like a fishing line. I was about to take the bait.

"Okay. Twenty-five."

I imagined what it would be like to be on the receiving end of this butch number. A charge shot through my groin. I didn't believe the girlfriend story for a minute. Maybe, just maybe, I could squeeze in some time this afternoon. At $25 he was a bargain.

"Wait for me," I said. "I'll only be a minute." Butch frowned, but I went into Matt's for some quick shopping. The store reeked of leather and incense. The smell only served to stir the sexual tiger in me waiting to burst out of its cage. I selected the best value in a leather ball stretcher I could find and made my purchase. The clerk, a well-built older man with a gray mustache and short dark hair thanked me and wished me "happy stretching."

When I stepped outside in the drizzle, Butch had disappeared, and with him the fantasies and remembrances of tricks past.

I felt slightly let down, as if I had been stood up for a date, but I brushed off the feeling and decided to grab a quick cup of coffee at a neighborhood café. I was in my apartment a half-hour later. I worked out for an hour with my weights and then, while I was making a bite to eat, I called Danny. We hadn't made plans for the evening, so it didn't surprise me he wasn't at home. I spent an hour or so re-reading passages from *The Crucible* by Arthur Miller and thought about Butch. I stared out the window across from my bed, heavy clouds were darkening the afternoon although the sun had not set. The phone rang and it was Danny. I told him to get his ass over to my apartment as soon as possible. Thinking about Butch had made me horny and I also wanted Danny to try on his gift from Matt's. I didn't tell him that I had a 9 p.m. appointment in the Combat Zone and I needed time to pick out my outfit and put on makeup.

* * *

Shortly after the appointed hour, I walked into the lobby of the Déjà Vu.

No one—not even Stephen Cross—would have recognized me. A couple of hours of makeup and a trip to the closet provided a look somewhere between Audrey Hepburn and Marilyn Monroe. Reserved glamour in a dress. The effect was perfect for keeping my identity hidden. Leather and jeans would have been too sexual, too suggestive—not that I wanted to go as a nun. However, for the most part, I wanted to be left alone. In the dark, as a woman, I would be regarded as one of the prostitutes who regularly visited the Déjà Vu. It was a pretty sure bet that Chris Spinetti would yawn in my direction.

My transvestitism was seen as an eccentricity at best, as an abomination at worst in certain straight and gay circles in Boston and, I suppose, around the United States. I had been around drag queens from the beginning of my hustling career. They were good people and accepted me when no one else would. After getting some tips one night from Ophelia Cox, a tall black drag, I ventured forth into this new personal landscape. One fact amazed me: I could put on women's clothes and makeup and no one recog-

45

nized me. It was comfortable to slip into a new personality now and then. My affection for women's clothing often provided a welcome change from leather, my attire of choice. However, as far as I was concerned, nothing matched the pleasure of a smooth slip against freshly washed and shaven skin.

The Déjà Vu was a faded theater in the grand tradition. The top vaudeville performers had played the house after its construction in 1915. The Champion Theatre, as it was known then, held 1,300 paying customers when filled. It provided expansive orchestra seating, a mezzanine, two balconies, eight loges, a smoking lounge for men, and a powder room for women. Gold putti hovered above the exit archways. Murals of verdant meadows filled with vines and flowers and lute-playing muses adorned the walls and ceiling. Before and during the Depression, the Champion did business as a first-run movie house. In its heyday, during World War II, servicemen and their girlfriends necked in the balconies. Business fell off during the 1950s with the introduction of television, and the theater fell vacant for many years. Then, in the 1970s, Boston's city fathers came up with the extraordinary idea of creating a "red light district"—the Combat Zone—to control the expanding sex industry. A group of high profile crime bosses took an interest in the Champion and converted it to the Déjà Vu. But AIDS and a crackdown on sex businesses were killing the Zone, and the Déjà Vu was its slowly dying heart. The theater sat on Washington Street, surrounded by the equally gaudy lights of Chinatown restaurants and gift stores. Several blocks away, deserted adult book stores were being leveled for a new downtown parking lot.

I paid seven dollars to a bored Turkish man behind bulletproof glass for the privilege of walking on the now stained and grimy floor that had supported the feet of Clarke Gable, Vivian Leigh, Spencer Tracy, Katherine Hepburn, and countless other stars. The Champion hadn't aged well.

A thread-bare brown carpet lay soiled and frayed in place of the kingly red runners that had stretched the length of the marble lobby. The gray and white floor looked greasy and tired. The walls, which fifty years ago glittered and shone in the reflected light of chandeliers, were now peeling, spotted, and drab.

Stephen Cross wasn't in the lobby. I wondered if he had decided not to come, or if John had strong-armed him over dinner.

I pushed open a set of double doors and stood in the blackness. I groped my way to a ledge at the back of the theater. Fifty feet away, on a huge screen, a woman gave a man a blow job. The reflected light from the screen danced through the Déjà Vu's innards.

The theater also smelled. The odor brought back hazy, half-crazed scenes from the uncounted times I had visited the theater before I got off dope and coke. The smell might gag a novice not used to its heady, narcotic aroma: a mixture of ammonia, smoke, booze, and sex. But, for me, it triggered an opposite response, one I had underestimated. I was like an alcoholic imprisoned in a liquor store and I fought the urge to give in, which triggered a clammy sweat. I imagined men with their pants pulled down to their knees surrounding me. Sex broke out in the seats in random orgies. Those visions left me shaky and frighteningly nostalgic.

I staggered as I pushed back the memories. As I groped my way down the right aisle in the darkness, moving toward a balcony entrance I knew was there, I touched a shoulder, a knee, a hairy arm. A chain-link fence now covered what had been a well-traveled stairwell. Sometime since my last visit, the management had confined all the action to the orchestra seats. I leaned against a wall and waited for my eyes to adjust to the flickering light.

Slowly, men appeared out of the gloom. Several gathered in a circle to my right in an area stripped of seats; other groups were scattered throughout the theater. The Déjà Vu did a good business on Saturday night.

My plan seemed to be working. No one approached me. I took a walk around, looking for Chris Spinetti. In the dark, I leaned a little too close to some of the patrons who made it quite clear they wanted no part of me. "Fuck off" was the catchphrase of the evening. Why pay for the pig when you can get the sausage for free?

A tattered red light hung over the descending stairs to the men's room. The whole scene reminded me of the gates of hell. The marble steps were steep and curved out of sight to the subterranean depths of urinals and stalls. I walked under the crimson bulb and wondered how unflattering my wig and make up must look under the garish rays. I descended about halfway, then took a cigarette from my purse and lit up. No smoking was one law—among others—ignored in the Déjà Vu. For several minutes, I watched the parade of men tramping back and forth from the restroom action. I was about to crush the butt into the spotted marble step when Stephen walked past me without a look. I glanced at my faux-diamond watch. It was 9:45 p.m.

"Hey, babe," I said in a deep, throaty voice, and thrust my hip against the wall. "Looking for some action?"

Stephen looked back, frowned, and headed down the steps.

"Stephen, it's me."

He turned, surprised. But his amazement quickly turned to anger. "Jesus, Des, I've been waiting in the lobby for twenty minutes. This place is scary. The guy in the booth was beginning to look at me funny." He eyed me from head to toe and scowled. "Some bodyguard."

"Don't piss me off, Stephen." I stepped away from the wall and got into his face. "I've been looking for *your* detective. Perhaps you'd rather do this yourself."

"Okay, okay," he said, and his face softened a bit.

"Then follow me." I struck off up the stairs and into the theater. I had already covered the right side of the seating, so I veered left, acting as Stephen's advanced guard. Midway down the left aisle, I saw a profile I recognized. He was sitting alone. I motioned for Stephen to step in front of me. He resisted and I pushed him forward.

"You don't think that's Chris, do you?" Stephen asked in a whisper. "I can't really tell. My eyes haven't adjusted yet."

"Yes. Stranger things have happened. Remember the Hercules. Don't worry. I'll be right behind you if you need me." After another push, Stephen took a seat a few feet away from the man. Their heads turned toward each other. It was nearly impossible in the Déjà Vu murk to recognize a face more than four feet away. The going would be tricky now. I moved into the row behind, three seats down, hoping to insinuate myself close enough to eavesdrop on a conversation without giving away my presence.

The man looked back as I sat, I turned my head quickly to the right. When I looked again, he was bent over, his head bowed. A lighter flared as he lit a cigarette, and I recognized Chris Spinetti. Even cops broke the law. I slid a seat closer to them and hoped I could hear their conversation over the orgiastic soundtrack. Stephen moved next to the detective.

"Chris?" I heard Stephen ask.

The detective jumped in his seat. "What the fuck! Where's your head!"

The theater quieted. Stephen lowered his head like a chastised kindergartner. I scrunched down in my seat as far as my dress would let me go.

Chris took a drag on his cigarette. The red tip fired like hot coals and then diminished to an amber glow.

"Sorry," Stephen said meekly.

"*Sorry?*" Chris mumbled something that sounded like "you could have been shot," and then shook his head.

"I need to talk," Stephen continued. "I figured you might be here—working."

Their voices lowered and I strained to hear the conversation, first from Chris.

". . . hell of a life working porn theaters, baiting a psycho...."

Stephen nodded. Over the next ten minutes, their conversation drifted in and out of my ears, but I heard Stephen mention some neo-Nazi group I'd never heard, and then tell his tale of woe concerning Rodney Jessup, including Stephen's admission that he had a business card from Jessup that Rodney had written on when they were meeting at the Hercules. It was in his apartment now, downstairs filed with some old papers, Stephen told him. There was also the small issue of a half-a-million dollar bounty on his head.

I leaned forward.

Chris snickered. "When you swing your dick around, something's bound to get hit. Quite a story. So, you think he wants you dead."

"Who knows? I've made plenty of enemies, but I tried to get in touch with Rodney when I found out he was running for President. He won't return my calls. I'm sure he knows who I am. How could he have forgotten? I'm thinking about going public—outing him—"

The screen erupted in the simultaneous orgasm of two men and a woman, a messy threesome.

"*Shit!*" A pair of icy hands pushed my legs apart. A thin snake of a man had wriggled his way down the aisle and planted his face in front of my lap. I had been so engrossed in the conversation I hadn't noticed. I slapped his hands away.

The moment I shouted, I knew I was in trouble. It was an instinctive reaction based on surprise. I clamped my hand over my mouth, but it was too late. The snake slithered away in the dark while Chris rose like a cobra from his seat. He turned with a gaze as fixed and accurate as a laser. His eyes practically burned with rage.

"As I fucking live and breathe...Desdemona."
I rippled the fingers of my right hand in a wave.
Stephen sighed and sunk into his seat.

CHAPTER SEVEN

THE EXPRESSION ON CHRIS'S FACE COULD HAVE curdled milk.

He was as cocky as ever, in his mid thirties, good looking, and athletic. The women at District Four, who swooned over his pencil sharpening, dubbed him "Spaghetti Spinetti" referring to his birth in Boston's Italian North End, and the rumored likeness, long and thin, of his prominent family jewel. His dark hair and eyes and full black mustache garnered Chris more than his share of sexual opportunity with women. Opportunistic men had to wait in line. He had fathered two daughters, and then more than a year ago, after ten years of marriage, his wife divorced him. The rumors started then: stories of Chris haunting tearooms, cruise areas, the Zone, all in the name of police work.

Chris came down hard on me when I was shot. He was sure the case was more than small-time robbery (my story) and he was right. I was trying to score. I could see the low-life scum look aimed at me. He questioned me in the hospital until I prayed for an over-dose of Percocet—anything to stop the chatter in my brain. Then he tried baiting me. He was sure I was a dealer, and he knew my contacts, etc., etc. I had sold to my drug-using friends small-time, not to make a living. Chris didn't like me—he made that clear— and he was eager to escort me, at my earliest fuck up, to the nearest slat house. I sensed there was more to his anger than just a desire to rid Boston streets of drugs. Call it intuition, prophecy, whatever you want—Chris was angry with me because I was gay. I was too much of a homosexual for his tastes. An over-the-top queen who didn't give a fuck about anyone else's opinion. I could see it in his angry eyes as I sweated in my hospital bed.

There was a rumored darker side to Chris, too—whispered secrets on the street. I tried to persuade Stephen that Chris wasn't the Jesus figure he imagined, but Stephen's mind was made up. My somewhat naïve journalist friend liked Chris's ego stroking: the easy charm Chris could display when needed, the flirtation and compliments, the solid-working class, no-bullshit attitude. But all was not right in the world of Chris Spinetti and I knew it. Chris's divorce had been nasty. There were tales of abusive behavior, presumably against his wife. The two girls were in their mother's custody, so Chris was alone in the world, and, as far as I was concerned, a loose cannon. Added to that were the rumors about his homosexuality, which from his attitude towards me, I judged to be true.

"Asshole!" Chris's voice boomed through the Déjà Vu. "I'm on a case—I should run your ass in." Several men jumped to their feet and rushed toward the exit.

I lit a cigarette. "How's the wife and kids?" I asked in a breathy exhale. "I paid my admission, just the like the rest of you perverts."

He reached for my throat, but then thought better of it.

"Cody, you're fucked up. You got nothing to do with this, so, be my guest, take a hike. Strictly business, understand?"

Stephen, sensing the impending explosion, spoke up, "Look,

why don't you two cool off. Des was the one who convinced me to come here. I didn't want to come alone. My mistake." Stephen rose from his chair and slammed the seat against its back. "I don't have time for this."

"Wait a minute," the detective ordered. "We're not through." Chris stepped over his chair and settled in next to me. "A TV on drugs is not your most reliable person." His shiny white teeth looked vampiric in the flickering light.

"I've been clean since I was shot and you know it. You remember—we had some tea and sympathy in my hospital room about my unfortunate mishap. After that came recovery and serenity. You ought to try it."

"I hear about the bodyguard shit you try to get away with. It'll be a cold day in hell before you get a license. I'll make sure it doesn't happen."

I pointed my cigarette in his direction. "You seem angry, Chris. You got a bad case of the coming out blues?"

"What are you saying?"

"Enough," Stephen said. "Let's at least go into the lobby where we can see each other."

We trooped from the seats into the dirty brown light of the lobby. I gathered my share of stares, the most disapproving of which came from Chris. He looked like a wild beast ready to kill, like a junkie without a fix. My black dress, blond wig, and faux pearls were lost on Chris. I crushed out my cigarette under the "No Smoking" sign. Chris lit another. The men leaving the theater avoided us, and those coming in gave us suspicious looks before veering off into the darkness.

"On second thought, it stinks in here," Chris said. "I'm leaving."

Stephen grabbed him by the arm. "Two men are dead. This whacko may be after me. Des dragged me down here because *I*— you got it?—*I* want *you* and your police buddies to do something.

You won't come to me, I'll come to you. I don't want to end up in the morgue." He pointed to me. "Des, you might as well hear this, too. I'm getting death threats. More than one, in the mail, on the phone. I'm paying attention and I'm getting scared. Could be Rodney Jessup. Could be a neo-Nazi group like Aryan America. Could be a lone psycho. I need your help." Stephen leaned against the grimy wall. His shoulders sagged and his mouth turned down in the tired light.

"Relax," Chris said. He sounded a bit more civil as he looked around the lobby. "This isn't the place to talk—not good for you or me. I'm available. Call me."

Chris patted Stephen on the back and strode out past the bored Turkish ticket taker, leaving me to contend with a man as bleak as mid-January.

"Well, that was fun," Stephen said, forcing a fake smile. "The next time you convince me to visit a porn theater remind me to have my head examined." He wriggled his fingers at me, wanting a cigarette. I obliged. He lit up and said, "I've had my fill of this place. The movies look awful and John's waiting up for me." He pushed himself away from the wall.

"One question, before you leave," I said. "What is Aryan America?"

Stephen frowned. "It's not the Daughters of the American Revolution. I've been researching them for a column I'm doing. They're based in New Hampshire, a group of neo-Nazis. Some of the younger ones, skinheads in their twenties, come into Boston looking for trouble. In fact, I was thinking that you might be a good plant."

I laughed. "You're insane."

"You'd fit in. I don't. You could get inside...put those hate mongers out of business.

"*You* are media struck. They're more than hate mongers, they're thugs, possibly killers."

Stephen hugged me.

"Watch the makeup," I said.

"Stay safe, Des. Thanks for being here. Sorry it didn't work out tonight. At least I got Chris's attention. Call me tomorrow."

Stephen walked out the door and blended into a clump of men prowling the Zone. I was left with the incessant sexual gymnastics on screen. *Oh, Déjà Vu, ma maison.* The feeling was too comfortable.

I thought about Stephen's crazy Aryan America idea for about a second before I dismissed it. He could use me as his researcher and I could go along with it, half because of ego and sense of adventure and half because I might put them out of business. I might even be able to pull it off. I could resurrect all the unfocused rage of my youth and channel it toward my own kind. I could bash fags with the best of them; open the vein of Aryan America and spill out its bloody secrets.

I shook my head to rid myself of that ridiculous idea.

Maybe I already knew too much about them for my own good, or they knew too much about me. After all, a bullet had come cruising through my hall window about a month ago.

And, I knew Stephen Cross.

One woe doth tread upon another's heel.

Ten days after I turned 15, my parents kicked me out of the house because I was queer. I was one of those teenage statistics that you hear about so often. Not that my family was particularly close. My father couldn't have cared less about me, and my mother was consumed with making a living. My dad was disabled and angry and spent most of his time coping with depression. It was up to my mother to hold the house together. I guess she figured it was easier to feed two mouths instead of three, so she supported my father's rage.

On the eleventh day after I turned 15, I hustled in a porn

theater. A businessman from Westchester County smuggled me into the Pussycat Theater on 42ⁿᵈ Street. I crouched behind his pinstriped legs and moved under the turnstile. The large woman in a floral print dress who was selling tickets was too preoccupied with the weekly TV Guide to notice. The businessman got the blowjob of his life and I earned twenty bucks – good wages for fifteen minutes of work from a starving kid. I ate a steak at the Howard Johnson's on Broadway and then found a flop house for the night where I slept in a tiny room on a bed with dirty sheets. It rained hard during the night and I looked out through the ripped curtains to the street which was white, red, and green with wavy reflected lights. I also saw the bums and winos huddled in a subway exit and sprawled in the doorways of deserted buildings. I thanked whatever God exists that I wasn't sleeping with rats or shitting my pants because I was drunk or hopped up. Some bums were too proud to do what I did; but I wasn't. From that day on, sex provided me with food and a roof over my head and I was grateful. Sex also defiled my innocence, made me look older than my years, and gave me countless cases of the clap and crabs. Most of that occurred before I learned that a hustler had to take care of himself in order to earn big money. I also discovered condoms. I was proud that I could slip a condom on a man without him ever knowing it. Sex gave me comfort in my loneliness, boosted my self esteem, and provided a rush. Sex led me to alcoholics and junkies, to financiers and CEOs. Sex strangled my youth, yet kept the boy and man alive. I desired sex as much as I desired book learning. A young hustler's career is short. I worked as long as I could until I found other ways to make money. Dealer to friends. Occasional pimp. Sometime laborer.

I took a respite from hustling for two years. I ended up one miserable night at a home for wayward boys on the Lower East Side because I got the flu. Fortunately, one man, an ex-Catholic priest, who was a saint as far as I was concerned, offered to take me in. He introduced me to Shakespeare, Marlowe, Tennessee Williams, and William Inge, all the great dramatists. Plays were my escape. Many nights in the kitchen, we would act out the parts and then talk about what the lines meant. The ex-priest had been an editor and knew language. He made me write essays about the plays and then corrected my English. I was never happier. He made me understand the benefits of study and the worth of learning. So, for two years I wrote, studied, and learned all I could. But my idyllic little world ended when the home was closed and my mentor was forced to move away. I took it hard and I fell off the wagon with an offer of money for sex. Soon, I was back out on the street.

I did too many drugs and had too much sex over the years, but I was never stupid. I kept reading because some viral voice in my head kept telling me that I needed to learn from words, and most of what I needed to know was in Shakespeare.

I looked at the black silhouettes in the Déjà Vu and remembered why I was there. Not for sex, food, or money, but for the love of a friend. Who were these men that hovered around me? Were they sad, happy, drunk, gay, or straight? What about the married man from Wellesley in the fifth row? What had convinced him to leave his wife at home on a Saturday night? Too many questions on his mind? All these years he thought he was straight, until he noticed a neighbor showering at the squash club. Now he can't stand to be around men because he gets shaky inside. A trip to the Déjà Vu, a straight porn theater filled with fags, will confirm his heterosexuality. Maybe the American Dream is collapsing around him.

I bought into the American Dream for a time. But it faded one crystalline October morning in Central Park. I lost the dream of cars, white-picket fences, two kids, and Golden Retrievers. I knew him from the times I'd had to rough it on the streets; he'd been kind to me. I discovered him on his stomach under an iron bench near the Alice in Wonderland playground. I knew what it was like to be without shelter. His exposed skin was tough and red and his clothes were soiled with chocolate brown spots. A gray squirrel loped to his side and nipped at his right hand. I chased the squirrel away and watched the sun split through the buildings in the east. The park was as good a place as any to die. I alerted a jogger in blue sweats that my friend had died and asked him to call the police. Standing a safe distance away, I watched as the ambulance drove into the park, casually, as if in slow motion. There was no rush. This was someone homeless, without friends or money. Why not take their time? They put on their yellow latex gloves and loaded him onto a gurney. I decided I didn't need the Dream because of its inequities. No amount of Dream living was going to change who I was—a small-time hustler who worked the streets for money. However, I didn't hate myself. My determination to be my true self was stronger than the Dream could ever be.

Shortly after 11p.m., sex walked into the Déjà Vu.

I watched as the man I'd talked with outside Matt's Leather Emporium pushed open the theater doors. He was wearing the same black jeans, white T-shirt, and leather jacket with taloned eagle patch on the right arm. Butch lifted each booted foot with commanding purpose. In the smoky cavern of the Déjà Vu, the young man with the incendiary blue eyes strode down the aisle like an agent of Lucifer, choosing the men he would cast into hell. I followed within a few yards.

Butch scooted into a seat next to an older man, leaned to the left, and whispered in his ear. The man shook his head. Butch lifted his long legs over the seats in front of him and disappeared into the depths of the next aisle.

I lost him for fifteen minutes. I covered the theater, poking my head into places I shouldn't have. My mind began to play games.

I half expected to hear a scream—the knife plunging into the next victim. Was Butch the Combat Zone killer? Knives floated through my mind like an insomniac's sheep. Stephen's SS dagger. Silver, gleaming blades. I was getting spooked.

I ducked into a darkened doorway. The red plastic exit sign and background lights were shattered. I backed into a corner and bumped into a body. I turned, startled. Cat eyes would have helped, but eventually my vision adjusted to the extreme darkness. Butch was molded into the corner. I could barely see him in the paltry light that filtered through the door.

"Sorry," I said.

No response. I moved away.

He grabbed my shoulder. "You're a man."

"Sherlock Holmes, I presume. I think we've had the pleasure of meeting."

"This afternoon—"

"—Perceptive. I believe you stood me up. Now, if you'll excuse me."

Butch hitched his jeans. "I got another trick. More money." He stared at me. "Why do you think you're better than me?"

"Better than I. In that sentence, you need to use 'I', not 'me'."

"That's exactly the kind of bullshit I mean. Better than us hustlers. Talking like you're a fucking English major. You're working this place, too."

"Not exactly. But if I was, you couldn't see me for the crowd."

"You got that twenty-five?"

"Not on me. I don't carry wads, least of all cash, to the Déjà Vu." I pressed closer to Butch. The moment our intimacy started to heat up, the sex hounds descended. Three men walked out of the darkness and surrounded us like hyenas anticipating a kill. Testosterone was thick in the air. I asked them politely to move away and they retreated. Prickles of excitement skittered across my skin. I thrust my hips against his, ran my hands over the firm stomach and pectorals underneath his shirt. I should have resisted, but I couldn't. "How's your girlfriend?" I whispered.

Butch shoved me from the corner and sent me hurtling into a row of seats. The back of my thighs struck a wooden armrest as my heels went out from under me. I caught the top of a vacant seat to keep from tumbling backwards into the chairs. My tight dress worked against me, and I struggled not to fall. I yelled and kicked into the darkness, but he was gone.

"Shit," I said to the shadows. The back of my legs stung and my dress was ripped about two inches below my ass. I saw a flashlight swinging down the aisle. It was time to exit before the manager made the decision for me. I held the back of my dress together and walked out. A depressing mist swirled around me as I hailed a cab at the corner of Essex and Washington Street. When I arrived home, I gave the driver my strand of faux pearls as collateral while I ran into the apartment to get $10. A quarter of a jar of cold cream later, I was in bed, rubbing the back of my legs.

* * *

Four loud knocks awakened me from a heavy sleep just after 2:30 a.m. The pounding on my metal door seemed like a dream at first—then the knocks came louder, harder. I was naked and sluggish, but bright enough to grab an iron fireplace poker I kept under my bed for just such an occasion. I snatched a towel from the bathroom, wrapped it around me, and barely missed stepping on my favorite Lena Horne album as I stumbled to the door.

"Who is it?" I asked.

No answer.

"I'm not opening the door until I know who's there." I wasn't worried about forced entry. My door was triple locked on the frame and police-bar secured from the floor. Feet shuffled in the hall and a shadow blotted out the crack of light under the door. A shiver ran over me.

"Please open the door." It sounded like Butch, although the voice was cracked and dry and barely above a whisper.

"How the fuck did you get in?" I was pissed now and heat rose in my face.

"Someone left. I came in."

Damn neighbors. I unlocked the door and opened it a crack, but kept the chain lock on. The unprotected bulb in the hall glared down. Butch was slumped on the floor near the window. Blood had caked from a cut on his upper lip and his right eye was purple and puffy. I was ready to take the poker to the other side of his face to even him out. "Spying on me? How did you know I live here?"

"Let me in," he pleaded. "I knew you lived here. I've seen you." He crawled toward the door.

I thrust the poker through the crack.

He stopped.

"Fuck you," I said. "I don't play games. You've got ten seconds to get out of here, otherwise the cops come." I slammed the door shut.

"Wait, Cody...."

I froze. He knew my name.

I grasped the poker and crept to the door. As quietly as I could, I disengaged the chain and swung open the door. He was standing in the hall like I was going to invite him in. I grabbed his jacket and slammed him into the wall. I brought the poker down on his windpipe and jammed my knee in his crotch.

"I'm not in the phone book," I said. "Talk. Now!"

His face contorted; he tried to speak and couldn't. I eased off on the poker, but lodged my knee tighter against his testicles. My towel slipped off my waist.

"Let me go," he sputtered. "I won't bother you."

"You're fucking right you won't because I'll have your balls on a plate if you so much as move."

He turned his head to the left, so I got the full effect of the beating he had taken. I felt slightly sorry for him.

"I've been in a fight. I feel sick."

"How do you know me?"

"I lived down the street at number 91. Thought I recognized you this afternoon. I remembered at the Déjà Vu."

I didn't believe him for a moment. I knew everyone in this neighborhood except the shut-ins; such a hot number would have been extremely visible on the street. I was certain he had followed me. "You've got a good memory—maybe too good."

I was naked and vulnerable. I stepped back, sliding the poker under his ribcage. "Open your jacket," I commanded. I patted him down. No weapon. "Hands up. Turn around slowly." He obeyed. I positioned the poker at the base of his spine. I ran my left hand over his body. My fingers stopped on the three-and-a-half inch handle of a three-bladed Browning field knife wedged between his boot and left pants leg. I thrust my hand under the cuff of his jeans, pulled out the knife and dropped it on the floor when I saw the blood on the handle. I needed to get my finger-prints off the knife.

I backed away. Except for the knife, he was clean. "Okay. Inside, but be careful. Don't step on the records."

Butch wove around the dustcovers on the floor and collapsed into a chair across from the bed. I switched on the overhead lights and pulled on a pair of gym shorts. Butch watched me blearily, unconcerned by my nakedness.

"Got any dope" he asked?

"Don't do it. What do you want?"

"I came to collect on our deal."

I laughed. "Now? You want me to pay you $25 to have sex now?" All I could think of was blood-spattered Emery after Alan punched him in *The Boys in the Band*. "You are definitely not ready for your close up."

Butch looked perplexed and shook his groggy head. "I need the money."

"You're a bloody mess and I need my sleep."

"I'll take a shower. We'll sleep together. Can I have a smoke?"

I tossed him the Marlboros from the coffee table and settled on the bed with the poker by my side.

"It was a good fight," he said and then lit the smoke. "Assholes called me a faggot."

"Do you have any sweet Jesus idea what's been going on in the Combat Zone? The murders?" He shrugged, exhaled, and threw the pack back to me. I reached for an ashtray and lit up. "There's blood on your knife. Mean anything to you?"

He stretched out his long legs and stared at his leather boots. I leaned closer to him; his eyes were bloodshot and tired. My hand started instinctively for him, but good sense told me to back off. He wasn't like Danny, a college student out for a good time. This man touched me in a deeper way—he was one of the damaged ones, a murky inhabitant of the street. At one time, I had been like him; I understood his struggles. His taut skin was pale and creased with fine lines. The face was structurally handsome—wide, a bold chin, the blazing blue eyes the centerpiece of the picture. There was a small scar under the lower lip I hadn't noticed before and his nose was slightly off-kilter from a break. Under my questioning, he bounced his fingers on the tops of his thighs and shifted his feet. I pushed myself further back on the bed, wary of the attraction spreading over me.

"I didn't kill no one," he said, his voice spreading over with pain. "Stanton didn't deserve that. Everybody knew him. Stan—"

"—Stanton? Was that the kid from Dorchester who was murdered recently? He was a hustler?"

"Sort of. He tricked some—not much. He needed money for college. We talked sometimes. He was nice."

I stared at him. Despite the cut and the puffy eye, he seemed physically unaffected by his injuries. It was obvious he'd smoked a joint or two.

"Sometimes johns get rough," he said, reading my look. "The blood's mine. A fight once in a while is part of the game."

"Nobody called you a faggot?"

He looked away from me. "No."

"What else have you lied about?"

"Okay, a few things, but I'm no fag. I'd seen you around. I followed your cab. Tougher to get inside. There's a flyer on the stairs with your name on it and C. Harper on the mailbox. I took a chance."

Butch was a decent detective. "I thought so. You're a little defensive about your girlfriend, aren't you?"

"Sorry. I hate it when people make fun of me, when they think they're better than me."

I had to admit, I had used a tone of superiority with him at the Déjà Vu. I handed him the ashtray and he crushed out his cigarette. I gave him another and he lit it. I walked to the sink and doused a paper towel with water. He pressed it to the cut and the wet paper bled pink.

"When you need money, you do what you have to," he said. "I got no parents. Ran away from a foster home in Albany. Boston seemed like the place to go. I thought I'd spend summers on the beach, but there ain't no fucking good beach in Boston." He took off his jacket. A blue tattoo popped out over his right wrist. I read two words written in flowery script: *Aryan America*.

I made no attempt to conceal my curiosity. "Aryan America. What's that?"

"Used to belong. Not now. I left. Things got too personal."

"They figure you out?"

He jerked his head up. For an instant, hell burned in his eyes. "Carl, Adam, Hugh, the others, they were my family. The best I ever had. They treated me like something other than a piece of shit. They bailed me out in Michigan. I was only doing what they said. Beat up a couple of black guys. Nothing against them, I was just doing my job for the family. Carl, he was like my father. His son, Adam, was like my little brother. Carl taught me what I needed to know. He loved me, gave me money. Fixed me up with Jule, this girl from South Dakota. I was lonely as hell before I met Carl. Spent some time in jail for assault. You don't know how lonely life can be until you're in jail."

A full life for someone I judged to be no more than twenty-five.

"That's all," he said matter-of-factly.

"Tell me more."

Butch drew in his long legs. "Pay me."

"How much?"

"Twenty more."

"Done. Go ahead."

He took off his jacket and threw it on the bed. He pulled his T-shirt out of his jeans and ran his palms over his lean stomach. "Jule Percy was her name. I loved Jule. Long brown hair, beautiful blue eyes. Hugh, this guy my age, fell in love with her too. I met Hugh near the Zone one night handing out White Power stuff. He was doing what Carl told him. The next day he took me to New Hampshire to meet Carl and it was like Carl adopted me. Called me his lost son, just like the story in the Bible, he said. Carl was a father to every guy, but he especially liked Hugh and me because he figured we knew how to keep our asses clean. Whatever Carl said, we did."

"Even if it came to beating up blacks and queers."

"Couple of times."

Butch's eyes never waivered as he explained his past. I got the idea he could easily be a killer if pressed into service. He dabbed the paper towel on his lip. I got an ice cube for his eye.

"We were all close at the compound in New Hampshire," he continued. "A real family, but that was when things went bad. I'd see Jule with Hugh sometimes. They'd be talking and it'd bother me. Then I'd wake up at night and she'd be gone. She'd say she had gone for a walk, but I knew the truth. I could smell spunk on her. I took it a couple of times, but one morning just before dawn she woke me up. I could smell Hugh on her and I hit her – hard. When Hugh found out, he said he'd kill me. But before anything could happen, Carl stepped in. He said it wasn't good for the sons of Aryan America to fight each other. Not over a woman. 'Stick to the rules,' he said. That night when I went back to my cabin, Jule and all her stuff was gone. I never knew where."

He stripped off his shirt; his chest was hairless and his stomach thin, but packed with a ripple of muscles underneath. His nipples were brown and large.

"What about Hugh?" I asked.

Butch swiped his shirt across his chest. "Hugh hated me from then on. He told Carl that he met me in the Zone, that I was turning tricks, that I was a fag. So, Carl tried to 'convert' me, teach me how to be a man. But that pissed me off, and I told Carl it wasn't true, so he dropped it. Hugh still hated me because of Jule and he told Carl that *I* was after *him*. One night after dinner at the compound, Carl took me up to his office and asked me about what Hugh had said. I told him that Hugh was full of shit, but Carl thought it would be safer if I left Aryan America because this bullshit was all over the compound. I fucking wanted to kill Hugh, but there was nothing I could do.

"That night I heard scratching on the screen and I looked up and saw Hugh through the window, grinning at me in the moonlight. He was holding something, but I couldn't really see what it was—I thought it might be a gun. Scared the shit out of me. I yelled and he ran away. The next morning I got out. Hugh's crazy."

I was astounded by what I was hearing. Stephen's research into Aryan America and Butch's testimony had piqued my interest. "Where is the compound?" I asked.

"Don't go there, unless you *want* to get shot. The family is all over Boston—I've even seen Hugh here, but he hasn't seen me. The compound's near Warren. Ask any of the hicks. They'll tell you where it is."

I jotted down the town. "I don't believe we've been properly introduced. Who are you?"

"Clay."

"Clay—a nice name. Very earthy." A warm shock jolted me. "Take a shower, Clay. There's a bandage for your lip in the medicine cabinet."

Clay rose from his chair and stepped gingerly over the records on his way to the bathroom. I stripped off my gym shorts and took down a leather jockstrap from the wall. I picked up a Japanese condom from the nightstand and then put it back. As I recalled, Clay did not get fucked. I sat on the bed, smoked a cigarette, and listened to the water run in my tiny shower. The faucet squeaked, the water stopped, and Clay appeared in the door, a towel wrapped around his waist. The purple swelling around his eye looked less puffy. A bandage covered the cut on his upper lip. All-in-all, he looked fairly presentable. He walked in front of me and dropped the towel.

"I'm no fag," Clay said.

"I know," I whispered. I was transfixed. Hard muscles flowed underneath the lean flesh. Clay's shoulders were broad and his hips narrow. A feathery trail of brown hair led down from his navel into the spreading hair of his groin. His uncircumcised penis was long and thick and hung, along with a hefty set of balls between two well-muscled legs. I caressed his thighs, then turned his back to the bed and sat him down so his knees rested over the side. I pushed his upper body back onto the mattress. I got down on my knees and rubbed his penis and testicles. His cock grew with my touch; the balls scrunched closer in their loose pouch.

Clay lifted his head and said, "Faggot, give me a blow job."

In the right situation, the words could have been a turn on. I didn't like them from Clay.

"Shut up," I said. "I'm paying you. Don't talk."

I lowered my head toward his groin.

My mistake.

Clay bucked up from the bed. His abdomen smashed into my face; his right hand pushed my mouth into his crotch while he grasped my neck with his left. His strong hands forced the air from my windpipe. My ears buzzed. My throat burned. I gasped and tried to wrench myself free from his grip. The world was turning red.

"I should kill you faggot," Clay hissed. "You're scum, a maggot."

The pressure increased and blackness began to spin around me. I opened my mouth as far as I could and bit hard, not knowing where my teeth would land. Clay screamed and his hands flew off my neck. I thrust upward with my head and butted him under the chin.

Clay shuddered and fell back on the bed. His penis was still erect as he went down. He was excited by his extreme domination. Blood flowed down from one leg. My teeth had carved a bleeding circle in his left inner thigh.

"Get the fuck out," I shouted. I ran to the bathroom, rinsed out my mouth with mouthwash, then gathered his clothes and threw them on his limp body. I had definitely sent stars spinning in his head. Clay moved slowly under his shirt and jeans.

He shook his groggy head and said, "I didn't mean to hurt you. Just how I get off."

"You need a good master. I'd think twice before I'd try that on anyone else, especially considering what's going on in the Zone." I threw $45 on the bed. "Now, get out."

Clay clutched the money and stuffed it into his jacket. He lumbered into his clothes as he felt his jaw. "Look...I'm sorry, man." He touched his leg. "You fucking bit me."

I glared at him before I opened the door and invited him out again.

He walked out of my apartment. I heard the downstairs door slam. I locked the door, retreated to my bed, and was consumed by a sudden shaking fit.

The next morning, I found Clay's knife, name engraved on the handle, on the floor under the hall window where I had dropped it. I picked it up with a paper towel, wrapped it in a clean cloth and hid it in my bookcase behind *Suddenly, Last Summer.* As I stepped away, my legs buckled a little and visions filled my head. Clay thrusting the knife into Stephen on a humid summer day in Boston, Clay carving a swastika in the stomach of a sometime hustler from Dorchester. Clay, a bad boy with a knife. But was he the killer? I didn't know.

CHAPTER EIGHT

JACK LIFTS THE REMOTE FROM THE WATER-STAINED
oak table and switches on the set. Sunday morning.

Black teenagers are talking about urban crime and violence.
Switch.

A muscular woman in a pink leotard performs crunches on a
Maui beach.

Switch.

A cartoon cat hammers a stiff cartoon mouse into the floor.

Another channel.

A simpering man in a gray sweater berates women who criticize their husbands.

A little longer on this one.

He switches to the local news. A benignly handsome man with
perfect hair and teeth speaks sternly about a riot in Los Angeles after a
neighborhood police shooting. The station cuts to scenes of the damage:
broken windows, the smoldering hulk of a car, a looted 7-Eleven. The
newscaster smiles weakly and proceeds to his next story—the rescue
of six black Labrador puppies buried alive by their owner.

"How cruel," the newscaster comments. *"What an awful story."*

Jack laughs a little, but the lump rises in his throat. He knocks it back.

Switch.

A minister who's running for President. Rodney Jessup is his name.

Maybe he's a fag. He certainly looks like one. Dyed blond hair. A tad too much makeup on the lips and cheeks.

Jack listens to the candidate: *"I want to quote from the Bible ...Romans...there are so many prohibitions, some direct orders from God. But we'll start with Romans, Chap. 1, verse 27. 'And likewise also the men leaving the natural use of woman, burned in their lust one toward another; men with men working that which is unseemly, and receiving in themselves that recompense of their error which was met.'*

"What do you think Paul is saying here? I tell you what: They burned with lust for one another and they got the reward they deserved. He goes on to say that their lives were filled with every kind of wickedness and sin. Greed. Hate. Envy. Murder. Fighting. Lying. Bitterness. Gossip.

"They were fully aware of God's penalties, yet they went ahead with their sins and recruited others as well. Paul spells it all out. What do you think he means? He is saying, 'good men rise and take heed.' We must stop this perversion, this foul blight from spreading."

Then the preacher talks for ten minutes about supporting his candidacy and where to send money. The squeaky-clean host thanks Rev. Jessup for his time and offers his supportive prayers.

Prayers. Success. Jack laughs because he knows success. He switches off the set and rotates the knife handle between his palms until it makes a tiny hole in the book he's positioned in his lap. *Mein Kampf.*

* * *

The wind rushes through the pines. The afternoon is cool and bright and he stares at the clock.

The slow afternoon disturbs him because when he's alone, and time crawls, the visions come. Jack digs under the bed for a pornographic magazine. He settles on the spongy mattress and fingers the pictures he's seen a hundred times before. One page he enjoys more than the others. He places the magazine flat on the bed and gathers the saliva in his mouth. He wets his tongue and runs it up and down the picture until the page is damp and curling. Whipped. Tied to the bed. He loves her.

His brother's face drifts into his memory.

"Get out," he shouts. No one hears. "Damn it. Go away!"

He strips down to his socks and shirt.

His father raised his hand, slapped his brother hard. The boy whimpered, cowered on the bed. Blood trickled from his nose. His father: big hands, square face, ruddy cheeks, a nose covered in gin blossoms. His breath smelled like booze.

Jack stares at the pictures. The end of the whip forced into her mouth. *Yes.* He lowers his head to the coverlet which looks like blue Swiss cheese it's filled with so many holes.

"No," he whispers to the air.

Another slap knocked his brother into the bed's footboard. The head cracked and his brother's arms and legs flopped like a dog hit by a car.

He spreads himself over the magazine. The pages bend under his weight. Jack wishes the man dressed in black leather would force the whip down the woman's throat until she dies, drowning her in her own vomit.

"You didn't see nothing," his father screamed at him. "He fell. The little shit fell." His head was about to burst with rage and shame. His father lifted the limp body from the bed—the last he saw of his brother until the funeral. Even then, he could not see

him or touch him because the three-foot casket was closed. He understood that people despised him. They stared at him as he walked down the red carpet, flowing like a river of blood to the casket. Some laughed. Some sniggered. Others vented their silent hatred and contempt, their mouths contorted in disgust.

His school friends shunned him the day after the burial. They yelled behind his back.

"Brother killer."

"Pushed your brother on the bed. Made him dead."

He ran home from school—the frantic beating of his heart carried him, his face red and swollen. The world denied him peace. Everyone: God, Jesus, Mary, his mother—dead for six years, his friends, and, most of all, his father, who can sit with him on his lap one minute and smack him to the floor the next. All are against him because his father told a lie. He ran past the creek where the milkweed burst with cottony spiders in the late September wind. The day was too bright, too luxurious. The sun burned against the small white houses. He was blinded by sunlight and rage.

He swung at his father who was drinking a beer in his favorite chair. The beer bubbled and spilled its frothy contents on the carpet.

"Stop it, you little fucker," his father yelled. "You crazy?"

He buries his head deeper into the blanket. Why cry? There are no tears left. The clock strikes 3 p.m. He writhes on the blue spread. The tops of the pine trees rock like cradles in the wind. Force the whip down her, into her, anywhere.

"STOP IT!"

No words came out. He cried and flailed, swung again and again, until his father kicked him to the floor, knocking the breath from him. He clawed at the air until his lungs grabbed a breath.

"You lied. You lied." He spit out the words between gasps.

His father was on him, smothering him with his weight,

74

*stomach pushing into his, their arms pinned together. The alco-
holic breath poured into his mouth and eyes.*

"You want to see your old man dead?" His father shook him
against the floor. "What the hell are you going to do if you don't
have me? What? Answer me. WHAT? How are you going to eat?
How are you going to live? Ever think about that?"

Jack drowned under the man.

"I'm sick," Jack said. "Going to throw up."

"Keep it down."

"I can't."

"You can if I say so."

His father curbed his rage, took in long draughts of air, and
lifted himself from Jack. He wrenched himself away, darting into
the bathroom and bending over the toilet. After he threw up,
he ran to his room and slammed the door. He pulled the blue
coverlet over his head and cried. His tears stained the bed while
his father drank in the living room.

He twists the magazine until the woman's head snaps.

Jack walks into the woods wearing his open flannel shirt and
white socks. The dead pine needles stick through the cotton into
his feet. The ground is moist from a little overnight rain.

He finds a one-inch brown beetle under the bark of a fallen
birch tree. The insect waves its wire-thin legs in the air and
pushes its hard shell against his imprisoning thumb and forefinger. He puts the beetle in his mouth and cracks down on the
shell. The barbed legs scrape against his tongue. A bitter juice fills
his mouth. The bug slides down his throat.

Ahead, Jack sees the gray cemetery markers. The air is chilly
and damp in the shady pines. He touches the slate markers; they
feel cold and slick. A low stone wall borders the graves and the
land slopes beyond into a gully. He steps over the wall into the
depression. What did he see? Light pops through the trees.

Flashbulbs. They took his father away a few months after his brother's death. A reporter and photographer from the city newspaper guarded the front door like watchful dogs. The camera flashed in the dusk. The sheriff begged his father to come out of the house, to give up. The sheriff knew the truth.

"Don't get drunk and tell tales. Every soul in this town was suspicious of how that little boy died. The coroner's report has come back. It didn't make sense until we put two and two together," the sheriff said through the megaphone. "Come out and talk." The sheriff put the megaphone down and asked his deputy, "How could he blame it on his own son?"

The trees pop in brilliant yellow flashes.

"Get off my property, son-of-a-bitch," his father yelled out the window. "I'll kill you! Kill you, him, and me."

The sheriff cupped his hands and yelled back, "Don't be crazy."

His father held him by the throat until his face turned purple.

When he came to, his father was bleeding on the sidewalk, the flashbulbs firing.

The sheriff patted his head and whisked him into the car, away from his father, the house, the town, everything he had ever known.

He steadies himself with deep gulping breaths.

A mound of ashes rises within a circle of rock in the muted shadows. He pokes a stick into the charred remains of rubber dolls, their blackened arms and legs scattered among the stones. The dolls twist and turn in sexual abandonment, but their rubber heads jiggle from their slit throats, their thighs peel open with tiny carved swastikas. The decapitated head of one stares into the dark woods.

Anxiety crawls over his skin. He paws through the ashes and listens to the low wail that has risen in his head. How long does he listen to its song? A second, an eternity? No matter.

"Faggot!"

His father's voice draws him away from the dream. The earth sinks into black stillness as ashes cling to his body. Jack lifts himself from the ground and stumbles out of the gully. It is cold for July. When he goes to the city tonight, it will be warmer.

CHAPTER NINE

SUNDAY WAS A BLUR OF SLEEP. AFTER I FOUND CLAY'S knife, I cooked breakfast, scrambled eggs and toast, and went back to bed. I took an old Valium to keep the dreams out of my head; otherwise, I wouldn't have been able to sleep. I woke up at 4 p.m. and raised the window in my apartment. It had rained during the afternoon; the leaves were wet, and black puddles of water stood in the gutters.

After a slow run through the neighborhood (hampered as I was by my nicotine addiction), I sat on the bed and took stock of the records, books, the knick-knacks, and other items I planned to haul tomorrow to flea markets and junk shops. Because Chris had paralyzed my efforts to get bonded based on my "background," my bodyguard work had trickled to nothing. And Stephen wasn't a paying client. So, I switched to plan B. I'd sell a few things to make the month's rent. If I was lucky, I'd get about $200 for my efforts, enough for about half the monthly expenses. It wasn't the way I preferred to make money, but I had no other choice.

That evening, I forgot to call Stephen Cross.

* * *

I was dressed by 9 a.m. Monday morning and ready to move the bundles down the stairs. Even at this early hour the sun baked Boston. The air hung like a damp cloth over the street. The afternoon promised to be frightful: muggy and close, not pleasant for schlepping my treasures around the city.

I had dragged one of my bags stuffed with records to the door when the phone rang. I picked up the receiver and heard the clatter of a computer keyboard on the other end.

"Didn't hear from you Sunday," Stephen said. "Thought I'd call."

"Pardon me, but I was exhausted." I told him in detail about my encounter with Clay Krieger.

"You are damn lucky," Stephen said.

"I know. My first mistake was letting my libido get the better of me. I should have put the kibosh on that when I saw him at Matt's."

"What was his name again?" Stephen asked. I thought it odd because journalists were supposed to remember names. He must have had other things on his mind.

"Clay. Clay Krieger."

"Don't know him, but Aryan America must have been trouble in paradise for him. Maybe we could take my car up to Warren tomorrow. Take a look around. Safely, of course."

I thought of Stephen's blue 1990 Honda Civic—dependable, reliable, and a veteran of New England weather and traffic.

"Maybe," I said, "but I need to make money today."

The keyboard stopped clattering and Stephen was silent for a few moments before he spoke again. "I forgot to tell you—you probably don't have any interest—but I came to a decision last night." Stephen sighed and I heard the flare of a match. John must have been at work.

"Go on," I said.

"Well, I'm giving a speech tonight at the Boston Inclusive Coalition Annual Fund Dinner. I'd like you to be there."

"You're right, I'm not interested." I imagined a steep admission price and a boring gathering of glittering gays.

"That's why I didn't ask you before. But the event would be on me. John is going."

I chuckled. "You still haven't given me enough of an incentive."

"Des, it's going to be a hell of a speech. I'm going to *'out'* Rodney Jessup." He stopped, tempering his excitement. I was speechless. Stephen sounded like a little boy playing with a new train set, excited about his toy and looking forward to his first crash. The fortune teller inside me foresaw dire consequences.

"Do you think that's wise, considering...."

"Too late now. I've made up my mind—*and* Rodney Jessup wants to talk to me."

"What?" The story was getting weirder.

"I told you I tried to reach him a few times over the past month. I wanted to interview him for my column. I thought I'd start with how the campaign was going and then pop the question. He finally returned my call last night. I could feel the ice over the phone. Nothing but silence after our introduction."

"The great and powerful Rodney Jessup. Did he remember you?"

"No. So, I asked him why he called me back. I said, 'If you don't mind, I'll call you Rodney rather than Reverend Jessup. You never told me your real name.' I only knew it because of the business card that fell out of his pocket. He told me he called because he responds to all callers, for the good of the faith—a pious excuse. 'We're all important,' he said. I guess I'm just one of the flock—the black sheep, maybe.

"'Cast your mind back, Rodney,' I said. 'The Hercules Theater in New York City—1978 or so? Do you remember?' He told me he didn't know what I was talking about. I responded, 'I think you do.'

"I told him I was making an important speech and his name would figure prominently. The tension shot up over the phone. Suddenly, he wanted to talk. He said the earliest he could see me would be Tuesday in New Hampshire after a campaign stop there. He hoped we could talk rationally; find out what all 'this nonsense' was about. So Tuesday, if we go up together, we could do double business—Aryan America and Rodney Jessup."

"Honestly, Stephen, this sounds dangerous."

"Don't be a wuss, Des. This kind of work is just up your alley." He stopped and I heard drawers open and shut. "I'd feel better if I could find that damn business card."

"The card's no proof. It's your word against his. Your trick at the Hercules might just have happened to have it in his pocket."

"There's a little more to it than that. The card has my name on the back, written in pencil by Rodney. It has my old New Haven address and phone number on it—a record that could be checked, dated, and verified. 'Hercules' is written in the corner, but not the word 'theater'. . . ." There was an audible crack over the phone as if Stephen had slammed his fist on the desk. "The graphite smeared. There's a thumbprint."

Bingo! He's got him, hook, line, and sinker. An adrenaline rush stoked me.

"When do you want me to drop by?" I asked.

"How about six? We'll have a nice walk to the hotel."

* * *

Sweat was streaming off me by the time I got back to my apartment after 4 p.m. In six hours of work, I had netted about $235. 32. I found the thirty-two cents on the seat of a Green Line Lechmere train in Cambridge.

I ate an apple, showered, and dozed until 5:30, before I dressed in the best pair of dark jeans I owned and a short-sleeve white shirt. On my way out, I stopped at the bookcase and took Clay's knife from behind my collection of Tennessee Williams plays. I wedged the cloth-covered weapon inside my left high-top boot. In fifteen minutes, I was sitting on Stephen and John's landing.

Stephen, dressed in a black tuxedo, opened the door and smiled. "Are you crazy? Why didn't you ring?"

"I was enjoying the evening before the real festivities began."

"Honey? What's wrong?" Another voice inside the apartment. John Dresser, looking grim and fumbling with a tux tie, appeared at the door. One look and I remembered why Stephen was hooked up with this man. Stephen Cross, middle-aged political writer from Kansas, who'd made friends and enemies in Boston, was little more than an average looker compared to John, the Assistant Manager at The Body Club.

John, at least ten years younger than Stephen, was the stuff of fantasies for gay men and straight women. John had achieved his own successful marriage with the gym. He was shorter than Stephen, blond, soft blue eyes, and in the prime of his physical life. His face was drop-dead gorgeous with appropriately chiseled chin and cheekbones; the skin, not yet reflective of encroaching droop, stretched as smoothly as canvas across the handsome framework. More than one man had attempted to steal John away from Stephen and their monogamous relationship, but all comers had failed. The two had remained together since they met in 1990, both devoted to the partnership. My only solace was they had not yet reached the "seven-year itch."

John worked at the kind of place I loathed: a club of floor-to-ceiling mirrors, sparkling chrome exercise equipment, and twenty-four hour dance music. Not a haven for the image phobic by any means. I'd take bets (despite my smoking) I could out bench press any gay boy at any gym, especially where the pretty ones had oiled muscles, shaved bodies and crotches, and the fuck-you attitude. Who couldn't figure them out? The transformative experience from sand-kicked-in-the-face child queer to gym queens. The gym gods surely would scoff at the rusty weights under my bed, but

I looked as damn good, as Stephen would say, as those $100-a-month lifters. I was short, packed, and muscled in a 5' 10" frame. All in the genes. A psychiatrist would probably say my feelings about the gym were internalized homophobia. But then, I think most shrinks are full of shit. What floats your boat is your choice.

A cautious smile spread across John's face. It had been many months since we had seen each other. He moved his right hand behind his head and made a tugging motion. "I like your pony tail," he said.

I gave it a yank as John stepped back inside. Stephen bent down and tugged on it as well. "I suppose some would find it dashing," he said. "Very *Pirates of Penzance*. I still think you look better without it."

"I hope I'm not underdressed," I said, ignoring the dig, "but this is my best outfit."

"You're fine. I'm only in this penguin suit because I'm speaking." He sighed.

"Having second thoughts?" I asked.

"A few. I'm worried about John. I finally told him the whole story. There was never any reason until now. Rodney was one of those mysterious romances, a nova that exploded and then disappeared, that so many of us have in our histories. I could never have imagined that it would end up like this." Stephen looked past the trees into a hazy blue sky. Wistfully, if I had to guess. "John's concerned. And he knows that when you and I go out *we* always get into trouble. I told him about tomorrow." Stephen patted my head as if I were the faithful dog who had returned after running away. "I love that you're here, Des. I know you'll take care of me." He pounded his fists into his black cummerbund. "Damn, I wish I didn't have this gut."

"Love has a way of doing that," I said, looking down at my own flat stomach. "It's not that bad," I said throwing some flattery his way. "I've seen a lot worse on Channing Street."

Stephen sloughed off my compliment. "I spent the afternoon finishing my speech. It's more sympathetic than I imagined. Rodney made a great first impression. I discovered something today that I knew but wasn't ready to admit. I was in love with the guy all those years ago. Maybe a shrink would call it an obsession, a first crush, but it felt like love to me."

He sat next to me on the step and we laughed.

"If you loved him, why are you outing him?" I asked.

"Because I can't stand what he's become. How he *hates* us. There's more to it, but I can't go into it right now because John's here. Stephen waved his hands with a theatrical flair. "I broke down when Rodney said we couldn't go on. I thought the world was ending. I was young and stupid, but it was *so* painful."

"Well, Madame Bovary, before you reach for the arsenic, perhaps you should take a look at this." I took out the knife and unrolled it from its wrapping. "What do you think?"

"Jesus, Des, what am I supposed to think? It looks deadly."

I formed a trampoline with the cloth and bounced the weapon in the air. "The knife used in your stabbing? The knife used to carve swastikas into bodies? A little gift from a member of Aryan America."

I let the knife settle onto the fabric. Stephen stared and his fingers crept toward his abdomen.

"My gut," he said. "I live with this goddamn scar every day." He frowned with a hurt sadness. "Who knew you'd get to Aryan America so early? The whole idea of writing about them is a smoke screen to cover my own concern—"

"—Where did you get that?" John Dresser stood in the door. His expression was a cloudy gray.

I wrapped up the knife and reinserted it into my boot. "Sorry, John, it's from an acquaintance."

John shut the door and smirked. "Certainly, no one I want to know."

Stephen looked at his watch. "We'd better get going. I'll tell you later about the knife, baby. Door locked? Porch light on?"

"Yes," John said sourly.

We walked down the steps to the sidewalk. I lit a cigarette and made sure not to exhale smoke in John's direction. Stephen looked at me with covetous eyes, knowing he couldn't suck one down in front of John. We turned north on Columbus Avenue and passed rows of sun-warmed brownstones and brick apartment projects. Traffic hummed around us. Diners sipped drinks under San Pellegrino umbrellas at outdoor cafes.

When we crossed a bridge over the Massachusetts Turnpike, Stephen put his fingers through the chain-link suicide fence and stared at the cars and trucks racing by below.

"I don't want anyone to get hurt, Des," he yelled over the zip of engines.

I stood close to him. "Don't worry about me. You worry about yourself and John. I'm a tough kid who's been through trouble, and sometimes I like it. My life's never been dull."

When we reached the hotel entrance on Arlington Street, we stopped under the bright red canopy. John entered the revolving door and stood inside as Stephen and I talked.

"Maybe you should tell Chris about Clay Krieger," Stephen suggested.

I shrugged.

"Think about it," Stephen said. "For me."

"Since you put it that way," I replied.

Come inside. We could read John's lips through the glass.

"If I decide at the last minute not to out Rodney Jessup, I'll be talking about theories of the genetic predisposition of homosexuality."

I faked a yawn, checked the elastic band on my pony tail, and then escorted Stephen across the red carpet and through the revolving door.

* * *

The Gay Nineties had come to Boston in the gilded splendor of gold-leafed cartouches and twinkling chandeliers. The hotel ballroom sounded like a 747 on takeoff. Raucous laughter, loud conversations, and the sound of clinking glasses rolled across the room in bilious waves, overpowering any attempt at refined conversation. Waiters in white tuxedos balancing crystal wine glasses on silver trays, snaked through the crowd to tables festooned with lavender tablecloths and napkins. Rainbow-colored helium balloons floated over centerpieces of pink roses. The dinner took on a surreal quality for me, considering the Spartan charms of my life.

I had no problem with the scrubbed and smiling faces or the clatter of dinnerware. What I couldn't swallow was the sense of dread which washed over me during this celebratory evening. I grabbed a glass of mineral water from a passing waiter. The drink's icy frost chilled my hand. The man in the vat from my dream popped into my head. I shut my eyes and tried to push back the sense of alarm rising within me.

I might as well have been in Bora Bora. Everyone seemed to be speaking doggerel. I followed Stephen and John through the crowd. The men and women they spoke with were unaware of what lurked beyond the room's camaraderie: an outing that could change the political landscape, a killer who might have Stephen in his crosshairs. Safety and security were as commonplace as the morning paper to the other attendees. Stephen introduced me to several people. I shook their hands and promptly forgot their names. They moved their mouths. I nodded my head.

An Hispanic woman and an African-American man waved from a table across the room. Stephen put his left hand on John's shoulder and guided him through the crowd. I made a supreme effort to focus when Stephen introduced me to Lucinda Martinez and Win Hart.

Lucinda, or "Luce", the nickname she preferred, was the gay community liaison to the Mayor's office. She was about 30 years old, bright and pretty, with short black hair and darting brown eyes. She wore a radiant red evening dress, silver necklace, and earrings, all of which complemented her dark skin.

I recognized Win, a tall, thin, black man, who taught aerobics at The Body Club, the same health club where John worked. Win was handsome in a charcoal-gray tux. Although he was probably no more than 28, a few strands of gray threaded through his closely cropped hair. I had faint memories of him from my bar going days, although I was sure he didn't drink. He and John seemed to be good friends.

After we took our seats, Luce told Stephen, "Two reporters are here to cover your speech. I really had to work hard to get them to come with no clue about the story. Can't you give me a hint?"

Stephen smiled. "No, Luce. Patience."

"Your favorite cop is here, Stephen," Win said. He pointed to the corner near our table. Chris Spinetti was slouched against the wall, his tie askew on his white shirt. "Isn't he the straight one you talked to at the committee meeting?" Win asked. "Good thing we're an accepting bunch."

"Probably here to protect me," Stephen said, and waved to the detective.

Chris glowered and didn't wave back.

"Fits right in, doesn't he," I said to Stephen. "I thought protection was my job."

Chris was standing about twenty feet from the table. A man, identified by Luce as the founder of a gay and lesbian youth outreach organization, sidled up to Chris and chatted up the unmoved detective as we watched. Stephen put other faces to names: a gay city councilor, the head of the local AIDS-care group, a prominent gay attorney and his lover of 16 years, all to be honored for their service to the gay community.

Everyone had a cocktail except Win and me. Then dinner arrived—predictable hotel food, but of a higher quality than was usually served at similar functions. John and Win talked about the latest technological advances in step aerobics. Luce tried to engage me in dinner conversation, but I was reluctant to answer her barrage of questions about my background. I replied "New Rochelle" to most of her inquiries, which finally annoyed her. I was sure she would find out the true story later from Stephen and she would dislike me, but I had other matters on my mind at the moment.

I grew increasingly concerned about Stephen, who seemed, as the evening dragged on, to be withdrawing deeper into a funk. His conversation, when he decided to join in, seemed forced and a bit snappish. For the most part, he avoided talking altogether unless the subject was innocuous. Even then he stammered and appeared distracted. The pressure of his "revelation" was getting to him, I thought. John patted Stephen's hand and whispered to him several times. This small display of affection had a calming effect upon him.

After dinner, the BIC President, a prim lesbian named Kathy, who looked as if she should be selling fabrics at Laura Ashley, presented the community service awards. The crowd erupted after each presentation because the house was loaded with relatives and admirers. A few self-congratulatory speeches followed each award amid the bustle of waiters and clatter of coffee cups. Shortly after 8 p.m., Kathy introduced Stephen.

Polite applause filled the room. Stephen kissed John and rose from his chair. He leafed through his notes and then placed them on the table next to the lectern. He looked into the crowd. From our close vantage point, you could see the storm clouds passing across his eyes.

Stephen tapped the microphone and began. "When I was asked to speak at this dinner, I thought I would talk about a topic that's been in the news a lot lately—the theory of biological determination of sexual orientation…but it has become clear during the past two months, that I must talk about a subject closer to me—the response of the gay community to violence—the effects of threats made upon my life."

There were a few gasps. I, and everyone else at the table, looked at John. He frowned, lowered his head, and stared at the untouched cake on his dessert plate.

As Stephen continued talking about the culture of America's hatred for the homosexual, a few members of the community shook their heads in agreement. Luce fidgeted with her spoon and Win looked annoyed. "I was hoping Stephen might keep his speech lighter," Luce whispered to me.

As if in answer to her, Stephen continued, "This is no time to be coy. Once we were a queer joke, a laughable, mincing bunch of pansies with limp wrists and lisps. Post-Stonewall America views us differently. The joke is we graduated from sissies to destroyers of society, from Quentin Crisp to The Terminator, from silence to the destructor of families in little more than twenty-five years. The power shift our enemies have anointed upon us is monumental."

He paused and looked at our table.

"My enemies want me dead, but we are all targets. The subtle forms of hate remain: the snickers, the laughter, the crude jokes. Discrimination's still alive. What a tired word. Discrimination is the bureaucratic lessening of ignorance, hatred, and bigotry made palatable to the public."

He closed his eyes, as if to utter a prayer.

"Faggot, the joke.

"Queer, the laughingstock.

"Faggot, the threat.

"Queer, the destroyer of America.

"Today, the love that previously dared not speak its name can't keep its mouth shut and America is buying earplugs."

An uncomfortable rustle passed over the crowd.

"God, what's wrong with him?" Luce asked me.

"Stephen is teaching us to be diligent—to take nothing for granted," I whispered back.

"I have come to the point that I wish to address; the reason for my speech tonight—"

The sentence left Stephen's lips. He stopped and shaded his eyes with his hands. I saw his hands shake a bit; his mouth tightened and his gaze froze upon some object behind us. I turned to see a man in a blue suit walk out a side door.

"A moment," Stephen said to the crowd. As the glitterati chattered, he left the podium and returned to the table. In a strained voice, he said, "Rodney Jessup's here."

Stephen, John, and I ran to the ballroom entrance and peered over the brass banister to the first floor. The man Stephen believed to be Rodney Jessup was gone.

"I know he was here," Stephen said. "I saw him."

"I saw a man," I said. "Dark blue suit, red tie."

Chris Spinetti jogged up behind Stephen. "What's going on?" He put his hand on Stephen's shoulder. "God, you look like you've seen a ghost."

"I have—one from about twenty years ago," Stephen replied. "Rodney Jessup, just as I was about to—"

Chris bolted for the stairs.

"Wait," Stephen yelled. "I want him first. He's done nothing wrong." Chris cut short his sprint and returned to our group. Stephen kissed John. "Go back to your seats and tell Luce I'll be back in a few minutes. I'll look for him." His eyes were sad and moist. He left us standing at the railing and vanished down the stairs.

Luce and Win bombarded John with questions when we returned. The event chairman was already calling for an explanation. I waited until John was in his seat and I could see that Chris had returned to his position near the door. I excused myself on the pretense of going to the men's room.

I hurried down the steps, but Stephen and Rodney weren't to be found. I searched every red-tufted chair, the men's room, the gift shop, and the hotel restaurant where tourists in shorts and T-shirts dined. The hotel bar was the last place I checked.

The slim white face of the television preacher. The slim white face of Times Square.

I spotted Rodney Jessup sitting at the far end of the bar, across from a blue neon beer sign. The room smelled damp, smoky, and as sweet as brandy. The man I assumed to be Jessup was alone, sipping an amber liquid over ice from a rocks glass. I sat on a stool, two seats away. I knew little about him, but I decided to find out as much as possible as quickly as I could. I wondered where Stephen was. I looked around for him, my imagination placing him at a dark table, nursing a drink, watching Jessup, the too-real phantom he had conjured from his past. Stephen wasn't around, however, so it was up to me to conduct the interview for him.

"Drink's on me, Reverend Jessup." I pulled my billfold from my jean's pocket.

The man in a blue pin-stripe suit and red and blue striped tie turned to me. He was not the fire-breathing demon of my fantasies. Stephen was correct: the preacher was sleek, tall, handsome, maybe made more so by the muted light in the bar. His blond hair, neatly combed and parted on the left, topped a V-shaped face, culminating in a tapered chin. The proportions of his face and the graceful contours of the brows over the blue eyes defined a visual elegance.

"You know me?" he asked calmly. He lifted his glass and I caught a smoky whiff of scotch.

"Through a mutual friend—Stephen Cross." I lit a cigarette and offered him the pack. He waved it away.

He settled back in his chair and ordered another scotch on the rocks. I ordered mineral water with lime.

"Two drinks," he said. "That's my limit. Regardless of what Mr. Cross seems to think, I don't know him—have never known him." A light Southern accent glazed his speech, the vowels pulled tenderly before snapping into shape.

I wanted him to say "homosexual".

"I am a blessed man with a wonderful wife and two beautiful children. A rumor such as this can be very damaging at the wrong time. I came here tonight to dissuade Mr. Cross from making a rash statement that might result in a civil action, but I see I'm too late to intercede." He sipped his drink.

"He didn't get that far. He never said your name."

Rodney's lips parted in a thin smile.

"I meet so many people all the time, Mr.—"

"—Harper."

"I'm on my way to New Hampshire tomorrow, Mr. Harper. I would like to meet Mr. Cross. It's possible that we have crossed paths at some point, but I'm certain not in the way he recalls."

I took a drag on my cigarette. "How did you know Stephen was here tonight?"

"I have my sources and I also have a staff that reads newspapers—of all kinds."

"Stephen's invited me to come along tomorrow."

"You're welcome. All are welcome to join my campaign."

"Hate, Reverend Jessup. I'm pretty sure all I'd get is hate."

Rodney gulped his drink. "No, Mr. Harper. Love. You'd get pure Christian love. I don't approve of your lifestyle choice. Excuse me, I presume you're *homosexual*."

I laughed. "Nothing but. A finer specimen couldn't be found." Then I chuckled because *the word* sounded identical to Stephen's imitation.

Rodney turned to face me. "I don't really approve of the way you live, but I love you because Christ loves you. You and the rest of the homosexuals are wrong, Mr. Harper, because you want us to accept you. Love, yes. Accept, no. You're evil at worst, Mr. Harper. Wrong, at best."

"I can appreciate your position," I said. "You have your family, your career, your presidential credibility at risk if Stephen makes his little announcement. You can't stay quiet. Pay him off and your ass is guilty, even if you're not. Go public and fight it—proclaim your innocence to the great unwashed—the seeds of doubt will have been planted. Either way, you're screwed."

"Delicately put. This is the kind of twisted story a homosexual would make up about me. To destroy me. To trump up some fabricated nonsense about sex."

"It would ruin your campaign."

He brushed his hand through his hair. "The funny part is, Mr. Harper, I don't even expect to win the presidency, or even the state, the county, or the church down the block. I'm building for the future. I talk about the destruction of the family, drugs, violence, homosexuals, abortion, the threat to the one true ever-lasting church and I can see the fear in their eyes. They really believe the world is coming down around them. That's the key. They don't understand that it's been that way all along. But, looking at you Mr. Harper, I can see you know the truth." Rodney finished the last of his drink. "I must be going. I have a busy schedule tomorrow."

He extended his right hand. I shook it—warm to the touch—even after holding a cold glass. *Freezing. The vat.* He buttoned his suit coat.

I looked around for Stephen again.

"Remember, you're welcome," he said and then walked to the door.

He left me at the bar with his tab.

When I returned to the hall, the dinner had ended because of the awkward departure of the keynote speaker. Luce looked sour; she kept apologizing to the two reporters who were haranguing her. John frowned, angry and distraught. Win said Chris had been called to the station.

"This has been a first-class disaster," Luce said to me when the reporters left. "A sheer disaster. I promised them a story. Where's Stephen?"

"I didn't see him," I said. "I thought he'd be back by now. Jessup was in the bar alone."

John's hopeful glance faded.

"What's Stephen got to do with Rodney Jessup?" she asked.

"Patience, Luce," I said.

She scowled.

We waited for another hour. No Stephen. Win, John, and I searched the hotel, even taking the elevators to each floor in the building. Luce called their apartment and got the tape machine. The wait staff was clearing the tables when we left about 10 p.m.

"I'm sure Stephen's at home," I told John in an effort to soothe him as we descended the staircase. "He was embarrassed by Rodney."

John dismissed my lame excuse. "Stephen? Never."

John and I said our goodbyes to Lucinda and Win. John promised to call Win when he got home.

When we left the hotel, the night sky was hazy and thick, a few bulbous clouds already hiding bleary stars. John was sullen, unwilling to talk, as we walked back to the apartment. I was hesitant to bring up awkward conversation, so I smoked and whistled an anxious tune under my breath.

As we crossed Columbus Avenue, John finally spoke in agitated anger, "Stephen and I met on a night like this. It was after a poetry reading. We went for a walk on the Esplanade. The sky was just like tonight, warm and hazy. We sat on a bench and watched the lights twinkle across the Charles River."

I put my hand on his back.

"Our attraction was instantaneous. I loved the way he held my hand, the way he put his arm around my shoulder. I couldn't believe this intelligent, sensitive man could like me, much less want to go out with me."

"John," I said, "Really, you're going to trip over your own modesty." I wanted to tell him that Stephen was sure to be okay— that Stephen loved him and, of course, felt the same way about their relationship.

"No. I'm serious. I'd had a few boyfriends before I met him. When you have muscles, it's easy—but it's a blessing and a curse. I'd had some affairs, but I knew Stephen was different from the start. I was in love and I hoped he was in love with me. He told me about Kansas summers and I told him about Vermont winters. We both decided that if we could survive them, we could survive anything."

I had never experienced this intimacy from John and somehow the dark, the mood of the evening, made him seem smaller, less powerful than his well-built frame. We crossed an overpass and a commuter train rumbled on the tracks below. Above us, the street lights soared like little suns.

"*Stephen!*" The rumble in John's voice echoed the train, but it was filled with horror, almost rising to a howl. "I'll *kill him* when I get home. Walking out like that! What a stupid, stupid thing to do...getting involved in these groups and *politics*."

"He's okay," I said, not really believing my own words.

"The deeper we get into politics, Des, the more we become targets. Stephen and I argued about it—his taking on nasty groups in his column. He told me that politics is supposed to create waves. He said the country can't go back. I hate the whole shitty business...the media...fighting for rights...fighting for what? So, fags can–" He covered his face with his hands. After a few moments, he lowered his hands and kicked an empty beer bottle from the curb. The glass shattered in the street.

When we turned onto Channing, John knew something was wrong. The porch was dark – he had turned on the light before we left. As we came closer to the brownstone, I got the sense that things were not right at 308.

John ran, fumbling with his keys.

"Let me go first," I said, catching up to him.

"Shit!" He had the wrong key.

I tried to calm him. "Quiet. I know more about breaking and entering than you do."

"Damn."

He gave up trying to open the door.

It was unlocked; I pushed it open.

The frame inside had been jimmied. Splintered wood lay on the carpet; the security lock dangled from a fragment. I put my index finger to my mouth to hush John and then stepped inside. Wavy fingers of light from the streetlamps filtered through the bay window.

The sight was not pretty: bookcases were overturned, cushions were thrown from the couch, papers littered the floor.

"Oh, my God," John said.

I stumbled over an overturned floor lamp.

I heard a rustle, a quick movement downstairs.

"Is anyone in the building?" I whispered.

"The upstairs neighbors are on vacation. Let's get out, Des. We can go next door and call the police."

"You go." I wanted him out of the apartment fast. I pointed downstairs.

John ran out the door.

The rooms were ghost-story dark. My eyes sharpened, trying to detect any movement in the living and dining rooms; my ears sucked in any sound I could hear over the pounding of my heart.

I was in the middle of an adrenaline explosion. The rush pushed me on. I felt invincible, as I had many times before during drug-induced highs. I needed to be smarter. A madman, a killer, could be in the apartment. I centered myself, took a few deep breaths and walked on.

The dining room table and chairs were undisturbed, but books lay scattered on the floor around Stephen's computer cart. As I stepped into the kitchen, broken glass crunched under my feet.

The sound downstairs was unmistakable—the creak of sliding glass doors. I ran to the rear window in the dining room, thinking I might get a glimpse of the intruder in the alley below. A cat, flushed from its hiding place, darted for cover behind a trash can. Then stillness. I was too late.

I moved back through the mess in the kitchen. The counters were piled with canned goods and recipe books. Drawers of table-ware, kitchen utensils, towels, and pot holders had been poured on the floor.

The rooms below were unfamiliar to me and called for added caution. I thought of taking out Clay's knife, but didn't want to get my fingerprints on the butt. I retrieved a butcher knife from the floor and walked slowly down the stairs, holding the blade out and flat away from my body. The stairs led to a small room, an office where the intruder had had a good time. Books were opened, files and papers thrown about. The office was connected by a hall to a dark bathroom on the front of the building, but it was a curious bluish-gray light coming through a slightly opened door that attracted my attention. The faint glow arose from what I presumed was John and Stephen's bedroom.

I pushed open the door.

It was their bedroom. The room had been ransacked like the rest and the sliding doors to the back patio were open. Warm air wafted into the room.

The solitary eye of Stephen's laptop computer—missing, I now remembered, from the cart upstairs—sat unblinking in the center of the bed. The screen threw out the frosty light.

I looked at the three lines in large type emblazoned on the screen.

QUEERS BURN IN HELL

FAGGOTS

ARYAN AMERICA

TEN

EACH KILL MAKES HIM BOLDER AND HUNGRIER.
Now he can relax after the three-hour drive from Boston. The
man he wants is with him. It's after 1 a.m.

Jack sits in a chair at the foot of the bed and stares at his
prize. The man is naked, duct tape across his mouth, arms bound
behind his back, feet tied at the ankles. Jack scoots his chair closer
and picks up *Mein Kampf.* He reads the first page aloud. His
body twitches as he turns the page; a stringy, nervous high takes
over, like drinking too much coffee or eating too many Twinkies.
Jack knows he's lucky he got him. How smart to know the time
and place. Damn clever. How fortunate that his prize would step
outside the hotel, like he was looking for someone, as Jack waited
across the street out of security camera range. He knew the man
immediately from his picture in the newspaper column. Jack was
quick, around the dark corner, the gun against the spine. A quiet
walk to the van and the whole incident was over.

But first, to know this man…to let him know what he's facing.
His biological father would be proud. He's not the *little faggot*

anymore. He's a man now and men fear him. You can read any newspaper, tune into any news broadcast for proof. They talk about *The Combat Zone Killer.*

His little brother. The shroud covers his brother's body, but the soft, pale skin is visible under the transparent white cloth. When the shroud falls, the naked boy floats to him, hovers, and touches him gently with his hand. Touch. Crying and pain.

His brother disappears, but the touch lingers. Jack shakes his head and cries because the pale skin is a lie. His brother's face should be bruised and purple.

He lifts the man's ankles. Black hairs bristle against his hands. *Hate.* He pounds his fists into the bed. The man manages a muffled scream through the tape. Should he kill him? *No.*

Mein Kampf. Too boring. Books and more books. What do they mean? *The Fall of Liberalism, Christian Ethics, The New World Order, The Turner Diaries.* A three-foot pile of *Soldier of Fortune* magazines rests precariously against the wall under the picture of Jesus praying in the Garden.

The Turner Diaries is his favorite. Jack will read Chapter 23 to his prize—*The Day of the Rope*—and the man will understand why he has to die for the good of the nation.

The man sucks in air through his nose in tortured breaths. Jack studies the eyes—the man has the hollow, vacant look of terror.

"Answer some questions," Jack says and props his feet on the bed.

The man is still.

"Can you hear me, pervert?" Jack kicks the man's bound feet with his boot. The prize arches his back off the mattress.

Jack laughs and then asks, "Are you a man or a woman?" No response.

"Answer me, faggot! I'll take the tape off, but if you yell, I'll kill you." Jack rips the tape from the mouth. The man bites his lip to keep from screaming.

VINCENT WILDE

"Please don't kill me," the man whispers.

Jack remembers the voice from the night he stood in the alley in Boston, after his first kill. "Shut up. Are you a man or a woman?"

The prize laughs at the question. Jack falls on him, his hands squeezing his throat until the man bucks on the bed. "Answer me, damn it!"

Jack releases his grip and sits back in his chair. The man draws in huge, heaving breaths.

"Please, let me go. Look...I'm a man."

"Too obvious. Is your brain too small?"

A choking cough. "I don't understand."

"No? Don't you read *Time*? Are your genes fucked up?"

"No."

"Do you like being a cocksucker?"

The man closes his eyes and rests his head on the bed as if he's asleep. He coughs. Tears drop from the eyes, curve off the cheeks, and fall onto the blue coverlet.

"How can I answer that?" the man asks.

Jack ignores him and fires more questions: "How many perverts in your family? How many men have you fucked? Do you like shit on your dick? How much AIDS have you spread?" Jack stops, breathless from his fury.

"I'm negative," the man says.

Laughter. The man on the bed laughs, too.

Jack studies the prize. The slight paunch, the hairy chest and abdomen. *The adult. The man. The father. The hate.* His vision blurs, he winces and smacks his fists against the side of his head.

"Do I know you?" Jack asks as if he has shaken himself out of a dream.

"I'm Stephen Cross." Stephen lifts his head from the soiled bed. "Tell me what you want. If it's money, I can get money. Who are you?"

"You can call me Jack. Jack the Ripper." Jack smiles and says,

101

"Or you can call me The Combat Zone Killer. That's what they're calling me. Me and my friends are going to kill you—all of you. The pervert lovers, too."

Stephen drops his head back on the bed and sobs. "Oh, God. . . ."

"God won't help you," Jack says. "God's on my side."

Stephen's throat gurgles with little choking sounds.

"I like to kill queers," Jack says, "but maybe if you change, see things my way, I might let you live."

Stephen nods his head.

"So, you'll change?"

"I'll try," Stephen whispers.

"Louder."

"I'll try," Stephen says, raising his voice.

"Good." Jack squats on the floor so he can look directly into Stephen's face. "Do you like being called a faggot?"

"Sometimes it hurts. It hurts more than you know."

"Good. Good answer." He rises, sits on the bed, and cradles Stephen's head in his arms. "Go ahead. Cry."

Jack caresses the hair of the crying man.

"Cry."

ELEVEN

Emilia: *But did you ever tell him she was false?*
Iago: *I did.*
Emilia: *You told a lie, an odious, damned lie; upon my
soul, a lie, a wicked lie.*

I DREW IN A BREATH AND BEGAN, "TWENTY YEARS
ago, John, Stephen and Rodney Jessup met in the Hercules Theater
in New York City. They knew each other for three months." In
my mind, I could see the theater on 8th Avenue, the one I turned
tricks in so many times, the men huddled in the corner, hunched
in the seats.

John was slumped on the couch, his face in his hands.

"Do you understand what that means?" I asked. "Stephen's
a threat. He can ruin the reputation of a man who's running for
President."

John looked up; his eyes were red and swollen.

"Jessup's powerful, John. Even if he doesn't have a chance in hell, Stephen can still knock him out of the race. Jessup might fear extortion. Stephen could earn millions on the talk show circuit, not to mention the book sales."

"Stephen's not a blackmailer and he wouldn't stoop to tabloid journalism."

I sat beside him and put my arm around his shoulders. John sunk against my chest. I thought of the money Stephen mentioned. Half a million dollars.

* * *

The police from District Four finished their investigation about 3 a.m. After rousing a neighbor, John phoned the police and asked for Chris Spinetti, but was told he was "out of the car." The two cops who prowled through the apartment told us that Detective Spinetti was on a case and promised to get here when he could, but not to wait up, he would knock. As if anyone could get any sleep now. One of the cops shot me a lecherous smile, as if he pictured some early morning ménage a trois organized by the distraught host. The thought repulsed me. Every District Four cop must have known about the rumors swirling around Chris. The detective, if he was in the closet, was a ticking bomb: A man challenged by societal conventions and stereotypes, still coping with the frightening reality of his sexuality, living alone and poor compared to his married standards, loathed by a good deal of his fellow Americans, and, most likely, ridiculed by his fellow officers.

It promised to be a bumpy night.

The cops questioned John and me. We recounted the evening, including my conversation with Rodney Jessup. Jessup, of course, had the perfect alibi, being in a bar with me during Stephen's disappearance. One of the cops, Officer Handman, whose flesh ridged like a stack of pancakes under his uniform, pulled on his belt buckle and explained that a kidnapping "might have occurred," although he was treating the case as a simple burglary for now. If John wanted to file a missing persons report, he could do that, Handman explained. John, agitated and hoping Stephen would walk in the door any minute, dismissed kidnapping and paced nervously in the living room while the cops talked to us. John reported that he could find nothing missing. The only real damage was to the front door and a few kitchen glasses. However, the apartment was a mess. No drawer, file, or shelf had been untouched. The cops got fingerprint dust everywhere, but promised nothing in the way of results. They might find only the occupants' prints, they said.

The only clear lead was the computer screen. *Aryan America.* But the words could have been written to throw everyone off track. John had saved the language without disturbing evidence— at least that's what he thought. Officer Handman told John the computer might have to be confiscated later in the investigation.

After the cops gathered their information, they told John to "sit tight" and keep his hands off everything until Chris or another detective could come and conduct a more thorough investigation. Community Disorders would follow up, Handman said. He talked about the possibility of FBI involvement. John told them in a thick voice that he would wait as long as needed.

I wanted to go home, but John asked me to stay until he could get in touch with Win Hart. "The whole thing makes me so fucking mad," he yelled as he dialed Win. "I feel like I've been raped. Stephen hasn't come home and all I can think about is the fucking mess in this apartment. Shit." A few moments later, he got Win on the phone.

I understood what he was feeling: Security, comfort, and love had disappeared in one evening. Everything—the books, the stereo, the classical music, the fireplace—everything that had cheered them through their seasons together in Boston was meaningless now.

I walked to the bay window and looked out toward the hazy yellow light that rose above the eastern rooftops. Through the maple leaves, a few low clouds shimmered like pearls in the reflected city light. The room was in that strange time between light and dark, when objects took on a heightened dimension. The reds and blues in the oriental carpet gathered into liquid patterns as brilliant as stained glass on a sunny afternoon. The walls seemed there and not there—transparent and opaque at the same time. I clutched the top of the settee and felt as alone as John, or as alone as I imagined Stephen must be at that moment. When John came back into the room with a soda water in hand, I was shaking with fear. I turned quickly to the window and mumbled about the sunrise. I hated the Bay Village fortune teller. I knew Stephen was in danger, possibly dead. At least that was what I felt. I wanted to tell John, but I couldn't.

John leaned against the broken door frame. "I feel like shit," he said. He walked back to the kitchen and returned with two aspirins, which he swigged down with the water. He threw me a pack of cigarettes he'd found buried under the potholders, apparently Stephen's hiding place in the kitchen. I was dying for a smoke. I asked him if we could sit on the stoop and watch the sun come up. John, in his numbness, agreed.

"Skinheads," I said as we sat on the top step. I inhaled a deep drag and the smoke immediately gave me a nicotine lift.

John, still in his tux, leaned against the concrete stair well.

"The knife I showed Stephen came from one of them. Maybe there's a connection."

John turned his head and spit out the words savagely. "Don't even think it! It's not true. He's drunk. He got cold feet about us, or he's seeing someone else…something, anything."

I saw Win Hart round the corner at Columbus Avenue. He was the kind of man who looked jaunty no matter the situation. He bounced down the street, concerned but confident, carrying three paper bags in his hands.

"Soup's on," he yelled from half a block away. "Egg drop.

Guaranteed to calm you down."

John managed a weak smile when Win arrived. "I can't eat," he said.

"Eat," Win ordered. "I didn't call this order in at four in the morning for nothing. Voilà. Chinese breakfast in a jiffy." Win stroked John's head and then put the bags on the landing. "So, tell me what's up." Win pulled plastic forks and spoons, bowls and plates from one of the bags. He ripped open another and poured out generous portions of soup. John lifted his bowl and stared into the steaming liquid. Next came a carton of chicken with pea pods.

"Cody was telling me that Stephen may have been kidnapped by skinheads," John said.

"I didn't say that."

Win rolled his eyes. "Pardon me, but what the hell was all that crap about tonight. I thought Stephen was over the edge. Death threats? Was he serious?"

"Unfortunately, yes," I said.

"Get out," Win replied. "Why would anyone want to kill Stephen? I mean, everybody loves him. He's gentle, kind, and, no offense, an ordinary guy. God knows, he isn't rich."

"Money's hardly the object," I said. "There are other reasons." John sniffed and wiped tears from his eyes.

"Oh, God, John," Win said. "Forgive me. I've been an asshole." He reached over and gave John a kiss on the cheek. "Maybe we should go inside."

John pushed his plastic spoon into the bowl and the handle snapped. "The place is a mess." He turned to me. "I swear to God, Cody, if you know something, you have to tell the police."

I thought of Chris Spinetti and froze. John picked up on my reluctance.

"I'm talking about Stephen, not some unknown victim. If you don't talk to the police, I'll make sure they talk to you." Then, almost as an afterthought, he added, "Or you can find Stephen yourself."

"Okay," I said. "I'll find Stephen." All I had to do was look at John and think about the missing friend who meant so much to me and the decision was made. It was that easy.

"Let's go in," John said. "I can clear places at the table. Can you stay, Win? I think a detective will be here soon."

Win and I carried in the food while John went downstairs to change. Win's mouth opened as he surveyed the apartment.

"I'm glad we're alone," Win said. "Something weird happened while we were at the dinner."

I was all ears.

"A young guy, kind of cute, was hanging out at the Body Club about the time the dinner started, but he looked rougher than the usual types you see outside the gym."

"Who told you this?"

"Jay, our boss. I called him after I got home to tell him about the evening. I mean, with Stephen walking out and John being so upset...."

Win lowered his eyes as if he was embarrassed about the call.

"Go on," I said.

"Well, Jay said this guy looked like a skinhead—his words— short hair, long sideburns, black jeans, a white T-shirt, high-top boots, a swastika tattooed on one arm. Gave Jay the creeps. Jay wasn't certain at first, because you know how some of the leather sisters get off on that shit, but a swastika—come on. In poor taste, if you ask me, even for Halloween. Some of the gym queens complained because they were getting creeped out, too. So, Jay told this guy to move his ass away from the club. Jay swore the guy said, 'fucking faggot,' under his breath, and then gave him a look that was downright frightening."

I thought of Clay, but I knew it wasn't him. There was no swastika on either of his arms. "Did he do anything else?"

"No Just watched a couple of boys go in, like he was cruising them. Then he left."

"The BIC dinner was publicized, right?"

"All the gay rags, some fliers."

"Was Stephen mentioned?"

"Yeah. The ads said he was the keynote speaker." Win looked toward the kitchen. "Stephen's always been too serious. God, I don't want to upset John."

We heard John rattling around in the kitchen. He reappeared, attired in jeans and a short-sleeve shirt, with three bowls of hot rice on a tray.

We were all exhausted. At least Win had grabbed some sleep before John's call. We ate in silence at the table, and then, ignoring the cops warning about touching anything, settled in the living room after replacing the chair cushions. The room was growing brighter by the minute. I looked at my watch—it was a few minutes before 5 a.m.

"I should be going," I said. "I really need some sleep."

"Not yet, Cody," John said. "Wait a few more minutes."

"Where the hell is Chris?" I asked, irritated by my captivity.

"He'll be here," John snapped. "Go downstairs and sleep if you want. I can't."

I got up and paced the room. John put a few books back on the shelf. Win found the television remote and turned on a cable channel. An old John Wayne movie was playing. Win switched to CNN after a few minutes, complaining that he couldn't watch the slaughter of Native Americans in the name of westward expansion.

Slaughter got me to thinking about skinheads and Clay. *Krieger, or someone like him, must have been looking for Stephen for months.* I ached and my stomach hurt. I never used to ache or get scared because I obliterated those feelings with drugs or alcohol; but now that I was clean and sober, I had to face all the shit that life threw my way. It would have been very easy to walk out of the apartment and leave John to his troubles. After all, Stephen wasn't my lover. I really didn't have to be so concerned about what was happening to him. Who was I kidding? I cared a great deal about him and I was getting much too wrapped up in this whole mess.

I left John and Win and walked into the dining room determined to do a bit of detective work on my own. Stephen's empty computer cart sat surrounded by papers, books, manila folders, and letters, some sealed, some ragged and open. I attempted to be casual about my snooping. Nothing much on the floor struck my interest: bills, magazine solicitations, a letter from Stephen's parents, the usual stuff. The books didn't promise much either, except for one. It was a small blue book, but after I opened the cover and saw the handwriting, I knew what I had. It was Stephen's diary—dated entries that might hold some clue. I wanted this book before Chris or any of the cops from District Four got their hands on it. Knowing Stephen, he probably kept his diary a secret from John, who would never miss it.

I was plotting a maneuver to palm the diary and shove it down my boot when John, laughing maniacally, appeared at the dining room entrance. I casually shoved the book under some papers on the cart, hoping to come back to it later.

"You've got to see this, Des," John said, and then waved several pages in the air. Win, half asleep, looked up from the couch.

"Stephen got the funniest letter yesterday." John's voice cracked and then his mood shifted, like someone flirting with sorrow and joy and not knowing which one to settle down with for the evening.

"Dear Mr. Cross," John read aloud. "Because of your record of support for conservative causes, and your belief in the basic values of America, I am appealing to you to open your pockets in this time of need."

John snickered. "Once Stephen got a certificate proclaiming him a member in good standing of that *other party*. He ripped it up and tossed it in the fireplace."

He continued reading, "As our country struggles with issues that will shape it into the next century and as I begin my exploratory campaign for the presidency, I need your dollars and your support. We have achieved great victories, but the battle has just started.

"It goes on from there." John stopped and looked at me. "It's from the Council for Religious Advancement, signed, 'In Christian Love, Rodney Jessup.' When Stephen was reading it he got very frisky. We ended up in bed and both laughed about it."

I saw no humor in the letter and wondered how Stephen got on Jessup's mailing list. Was this a perverse joke, or an example of Jessup's warped sense of humor after Stephen's phone calls? Had Stephen's name been mentioned in the higher circles of the Council, or was this an error caused by some scatter-brained employee who crossed lists at a direct mail house? Or maybe Jessup dared to be smug because Stephen wasn't telling the truth. But why would he lie? Stephen had written plenty of damning articles—enough to be the target of more than a few groups. He was well aware of the risks and the enemies he made.

The buzzer vibrated on the wall and the outside door squeaked open. John dropped the letter on the mantle and turned. All eyes were directed at the apartment door just in time to see Chris Spinetti. Boston's most enigmatic detective looked as if he'd been up all night. He was wearing a white shirt and tan chinos, but the shirt looked as rumpled and creased as he did. Great dark half-circles underlined his deeply set eyes. He carried a black briefcase and a cup of coffee. The detective's mouth curled when he saw me.

"Stephen home yet?" Chris asked in a weary voice.

John shook his head.

"Filed a missing persons report?"

"Not yet," John answered. "The cops didn't seem to think it was necessary until after we had talked."

"Half the time, they don't fucking know what they're talking about." Chris glared at me and then directed his question to John. "Does *he* have to be here?"

"Yes. Only Stephen matters."

"Some interviews need to be private."

"Fuck privacy," John said matter-of-factly. "This is about Stephen and *we* need all the help we can get."

Chris took a few steps in and looked into the dining room. "Did a number, huh?" He turned to John. "Sorry, it's been a long night. We'll find him. District may put another detective on the case. Anything we say now is outside policy." Chris motioned for Win to move his legs so he could sit on the settee. Win complied, but not before giving me a look.

The detective withdrew a yellow legal pad and pen from his briefcase. "Could Stephen be somewhere else?" he asked. "A party? Drunk? Stoned?"

John looked incredulous. "Stephen? At six o'clock in the morning? He'd be home. He would never be *that* drunk and he doesn't do drugs."

"Got to ask. Has Stephen been out? You know, fucking around?"

John's face flushed.

"Look," Chris said. "Do you want to find him or not? A guy leaves a hotel and doesn't come home. Could be a million reasons, could be one. You've got to start somewhere."

"I understand," John said, "but Stephen would never do that."

"Just asking. Temptation's out there. I saw Stephen at the Déjà Vu."

"He went to find you," I said. "He wasn't *fucking* around."

The detective turned to me and his eyes had that beady "back off" expression. "What about you, Cody? You been fucking around?"

I took the bait in the detective's provocation. "I don't think we're in the same league, Chris."

Win sighed. "You guys are talking trash and getting nothing accomplished."

The detective glared at me. "What do you know about this?"

"Not much; however, the street does speak to me. Alas, alack, Chris, I like not this unnatural dealing."

"Cut the crap. Speak English."

"It's the King's English, Chris. Your problem is you can't see beyond your Hollywood face. The answer may be right in front of us."

"Then start talking," the detective demanded.

"It's nothing definitive."

"If you're withholding information, you'll be crawling on a cell floor with the rest of the cock...roaches."

"Don't be such a goddamn cop. If I knew anything I'd tell you." I stifled my urge to bash him in the head.

John interrupted our argument in a voice that rang out strong and steady in the room. "Tell him about the knife, Cody."

Blood rushed to my head.

Chris's eyes lit up like a man who had found the Holy Grail. "What knife?" he asked and for the first time he smiled at me.

John answered in a flat, unaffected voice before I could answer, "Aryan America."

"The skinheads?" Chris asked.

"Read Stephen's computer screen in our bedroom," John added, to drive the point deeper.

I saw red for a moment; John had betrayed me to a cop I loathed. I pushed back my anger—now was not the time to lose my composure. I didn't want to make up a story that would trap me later.

"A guy got into my building early Sunday morning. His name is Clay and he used to be a member of Aryan America—not anymore. He was a trick. That's all. He left his knife." I lifted it carefully out of my boot and handed it to Chris, who motioned for me to put it next to him on the settee.

He took two latex gloves from his briefcase, put them on, unrolled the cloth and looked at the weapon. A low whistle erupted from his mouth. I assumed dried blood got the detective excited. I didn't know what else he might be reacting to.

Chris leaned back with a confident smile on his face. I'd never seen him look so happy, glowing like a bride on her wedding day. "Clay Krieger, former skinhead, thug, hustler, piece of shit. Found in a dumpster a few hours ago in an alley off Tremont Street. Been dead about a day. His throat was cut. The Combat Zone Killer strikes again. I'm all over this one. Been in the Zone lately, Cody?"

The detective's smile turned to a smirk.

My heart skipped a few beats and suddenly I felt cold.

"Damn," Winn said and leaned forward on the couch.

Spinetti chuckled. I smelled "gloat" all over him. He folded the cloth over the knife, placed the bundle in his briefcase and closed it.

"Are you in the mood to travel?" Chris asked me. "How about a little trip to District? I'm going to look around here first, then we can go. Don't run off." He turned to John. "Got some coffee?"

"Regular okay?"

"Fine."

John, barely giving me a glance, brushed past me on the way to the kitchen. Chris nosed his way through the living room and then the dining room. I sat next to Win, who shook his head and plastered himself against the opposite end of the settee as far away from me as possible. The automatic coffee machine gurgled in the kitchen. I watched Chris, hoping he wouldn't pick up the diary I had stashed on the computer table. Chris, of course, had always been out to get me. Clay's knife was gold in his lap. I needed to formulate a plan—quickly.

Chris and John wandered about the rooms, coffee cups in hand, Chris smug and John reserved, talking about every item in the room. Their voices faded as they moved downstairs. Win scrunched up his face in disbelief. I was clearly not welcome on the same piece of furniture, so I moved to the chair. Since Stephen had dropped by my apartment to inform me of the first Combat Zone killing, I found myself on increasing occasions wishing for alcohol or drugs—in this case a black beauty and some speed to wash away my growing fatigue.

Win studied me with tired eyes. "I can't believe this. This is too freaky for me."

I waited for the next question—one he couldn't force himself to ask. I headed him off at the pass. "Don't worry. I didn't kill Clay Krieger."

Win eyed me stonily. We sat, silent, listening to the shuffle downstairs.

When I could take the silent treatment no longer, I walked into the kitchen for a drink of water. On the way back, I paused in front of the computer table—enough time to pick up the diary. I was fairly sure Win hadn't seen my movement, since he was looking out the bay window. I reached down. There was barely enough room to shove the book between my pants leg and the boot top. I returned to the chair.

John and Chris came back up the stairs about twenty minutes later as solemn as priests.

Chris opened his briefcase and dropped his pad inside. "I'll contact Community Disorders and file a missing person's report," he told John. The detective closed his briefcase, pointed at me and then the door. "Let's cruise, Des."

CHAPTER TWELVE

CHRIS TURNED ON THE AIR CONDITIONER FOR THE short drive to District Four. The morning was humid and the sun pale yellow in a gauzy cotton sky. The day would be hot and brown by mid-afternoon.

I walked out of District Four a free man after two hours of questioning about my relationship with Clay Krieger and Sunday's events. I had no alibi for Sunday night, the rough time estimate of Clay's murder. That night I was home alone preparing my stuff for sale. As I recalled, there were no phone calls for the phone company to log.

So, I sat in a slick green vinyl office chair while Chris harangued me about my past and my possible connection with a murder. The knife was all Chris needed.

How did I get the knife? I told Chris the story.

What did I know about Aryan America? Very little, I said. Clay had mentioned a compound in New Hampshire.

What did Rodney Jessup tell me? He told me he didn't know Stephen.

A minute more and I would have snapped. Another half hour and I might have killed him.

I walked out a free man because I escaped after Chris went to the bathroom. While he was taking a piss, I looked at the papers on his desk. Everything was pretty standard, but I did find a utility bill that listed his address—Carver Street in East Boston. I memorized it.

When he returned, I told him I needed to do the same because my stomach was "churning and I was feeling sick." I was sure, I told him, that he could commiserate because of the intense pressure he was putting on me. He scowled and told me where to go. Fortunately, the bathroom was next to an emergency exit that I was sure wasn't alarmed. They never are. I held back for a few seconds and then bolted through the door. I figured I had about ten minutes to do what I needed to do before my apartment would be awash in a sea of blue.

I pulled the diary out of my boot and ran, red-faced and puffing, to my apartment in about five minutes. I loathed being a smoker even as I craved a cigarette. I entered my building through the back basement door, twisting past the ancient washer and dryer in the dank, moldy darkness. I looked through the chicken wire of my green front door. No cops yet.

In my apartment, I grabbed my large black duffel bag, which was already partially filled for a quick getaway. I had stashed $958 behind some books. I grabbed the cash along with a carton of cigarettes, two summer dresses, a pair of flat pumps, two pairs of heels, my drag kit, a blond wig, my padded breasts, a padded panty for shapely hips and butt, and, most important, my reconditioned .357 Magnum I found in a garbage bag on West 46th Street in New York. My favorite pair of Crossman police-regulation handcuffs, a pair of pliers, a screwdriver, and Mag cartridges were already in the bag. I could have cried over what I was leaving: my books, plays, makeup, jewelry, records, leather, my weights, the special detritus I loved. I didn't know whether I would be back again, or if I did come back, what would be left.

Because I knew where everything was, packing took about three minutes. On impulse I threw my two-volume collection of the works of William Shakespeare, along with the diary, into the duffle, locked the door and headed down the stairs. At the front door, I looked out again but the cops weren't outside. I knew they would come cruising up at any time, lights on but no sirens.

I left the building through the back door and walked east in the alley behind Channing Street looking for suitable transportation. I couldn't ask John for Stephen's car; he would turn me in. I wanted an automobile that was common, but first I needed a license plate. A modest gray Honda sat most of the time in a parking spot behind the apartment building. Its plate was perfect, two numeral threes, which, with a bit of waterproof marker could easily be converted to eights. The plate came off with a few twists of the screwdriver.

I walked to Harrison and turned onto East Springfield. I knew hotwiring hands down, but I was looking for an easier mark. The cars on the street were secured with steering wheel clubs; others were alarm wired. I walked west to Tremont Street, dangerous territory because I was nearing Stephen and John's apartment.

The car I wanted—a red Chevy Cavalier with Massachusetts plates—was double parked with the keys in the ignition in front of Goldman's Bagels. There was a large crowd inside and everyone seemed intent on securing a morning nosh. All eyes were on the counter help.

I slipped behind the wheel and fired up the car, hoping the owner didn't see it slip away down Tremont Street. The owner might even finish a bagel inside before notifying the police. I wanted to be northbound for New Hampshire before the car was reported stolen. Traveling I-93 in a stolen car was an open invitation for a State Police arrest. A sandwich and a couple of hours sleep off the Interstate were what I needed, along with a chance to change the license plate.

About 10 a.m., I left the highway and parked in back of a convenience store lot in Woburn. I knew better than to park the car with the plate facing the store because of security cameras, so I backed in, popped the release, and put my duffle bag in the trunk. The back of the store bordered a marshy open lot (a former toxic waste dump, I was certain). I went inside and bought a turkey sandwich, water, and a green marker from a teenager who looked as sleepy as I felt.

I drove cautiously through Woburn and north into Burlington. After a few miles of serious searching I found a wooded area near an industrial park that didn't look patrolled. I pulled in and parked near the north end in the shade of a stringy willow. The sandwich and drink hit the spot. I colored the threes to eights on the Honda plate I had stolen and switched tags.

The car was stifling, but there was a breeze and a small pond nearby—those ubiquitous small depressions created for industrial parks. I stretched out near the pond with Stephen's diary in hand and thumbed through the pages.

It was more than a diary. It was a book of sketches about his life. *His life.* I dug my boots into the hard earth. What life did I have now? I pictured the FBI poster going up in the Post Office. *WANTED: For First Degree Murder, Armed and Dangerous, Cody Harper, AKA Desdemona.* I was banished from my apartment, on the run, because I wanted to find a friend who stirred romantic notions in me. Yet I already missed my leather, the posters, my books and plays, the small, comfortable realities of my life. I lit a cigarette and opened the diary. There were nice words about a mostly pleasant adolescence, coming out, lovers, and his first encounters with John. In a long passage, Stephen wrote about his first attraction to another boy and the difficulty of understanding his emotions. A few pages near the end were ripped from the book—the jagged tears along the spine were splintered and fresh. I lay back on the grass, unsettled.

* * *

"Hey buddy."

An unfamiliar voice lifted the black veil from my eyes.

"Wake up." The words came from a young man in a green uniform. "You slept through lunch."

I started, aware of my vulnerability, and looked at my watch. Half past two. I had been asleep for nearly four hours.

"Thanks," I said and shook the grog from my head. The sun had shifted beyond the zenith. My face felt flushed and burned.

"Saw you sleeping about an hour ago. I was mowing the other lot, but I got to mow here now.

I thanked him and muttered, "Back to the grind." Aside from a little stiffness, my body appreciated the sleep. I picked up the diary and headed for the Chevy, which sat shimmering in the afternoon sun. I twisted the air conditioner knob and hot air poured out of the vents.

I took the back roads, and by the time I reached Manchester, New Hampshire, about an hour later, the car was freezing. I didn't mind the goose bumps—air conditioning was a luxury.

I pulled into an economy motel near a large, glistening shopping center. The sun had dimmed under a bluish haze of clouds in the west, the harbinger of an approaching thunderstorm. When I stepped out of the car, the air hit me like a wet blanket.

A disinterested gray-haired man registered me at the check-in desk. I signed as Bryce Swerdloe from the Upper West Side, NYC, and paid $25 cash for a ground-floor room on the rear of the motel away from the street.

"What newspaper does everybody read around here?" I asked.

The man laughed. "You *are* from out-of-state. Only one paper to speak of—*The Union-Leader.* Gives you everything from picnics to politics."

He said the magic word—politics.

"Phone in the room?"

"Local calls are free. Long distance goes on your bill. Check out at 11 a.m." He looked down and busied his hands under the desk.

I parked the car a few spaces away from room number 11. I wanted to compose myself and dress before finding Rodney Jessup.

A drugstore happened to be a five-minute walk from the motel. I bought cream bleach, a copy of the paper, which, in large type on the front page, confirmed Rodney Jessup's appearance schedule in Manchester.

Jessup was meeting supporters from 3 to 5 p.m. at a downtown hotel and then was delivering a speech at the Holiness Church at 6 p.m. The last event was timed perfectly for the local evening news and also for me. It gave me time to dress and prepare my questions for the good Reverend. The paper mentioned a pot-luck supper for the candidate. Nothing suited me better than a free meal.

Safer in drag tonight.

I showered, shaved my legs and chest and applied the bleach to my arms. My hands and Adam's apple, the scourge of many would-be drag queens, weren't problems for me. My small hands and long fingers, with a light coat of makeup and polished nails, ensured a feminine illusion. My "apple" didn't protrude because of muscle thickness in my neck. When I was younger, I had considered the tracheal shave that many professional drags endure, but I never saved enough money for the operation. A silk scarf was much cheaper.

My makeup kit contained the basics, but didn't allow me to perform the kind of transformation I could have with the essentials I left behind in Boston. The stormy sky might obscure any noticeable faults. I started with a basic coverup, moved on to foundation, then to blush, eye liner, lashes, and lipstick. The eyebrows and lashes were the most work for me. It took a half-hour to get the blend that matched my natural brows. The end result was okay, but not gorgeous. I chose a royal blue dress I had pulled in haste from my closet. The dress, combined with the padded breasts, panty enhancer, and blond wig gave me a passable appearance. The navy heels were off but would have to do. When my drag was right, straight men stared and gay men worshipped. Tonight, I'd have to act as well.

When I judged myself as good as I could get, I left the motel about 5:30. I wondered what the desk man would think if he saw me walk out of number 11.

The paper had listed the church address. I found a New England map in the car's glove compartment and studied the inset map of Manchester. The church was a short drive across town, off the southern extension of I-293.

After a few wrong turns, I found the parking lot of the Holiness Church as large drops of rain splattered the windshield. The church looked like a granite square topped off with a steeple. I had expected it to be light and modern, but instead it stood severe and imposing on the top of a grassy hill. Four maples, in summer green, secured each corner of the lawn. I had a hard time finding a parking space, but finally found one quite a distance from the church. Radio and television station vans with their transmission gear lined the edge of the lot. A group of well-dressed men and women gathered around the church door.

I'd forgotten to take a purse when I left Boston, so I looked less the female. I locked the car and carried the keys in my hand. As I walked up the hill, I spotted a woman who looked official. She carried a yellow legal pad, which shone against her red dress. She turned from a group of reporters carrying video cameras.

"Excuse me," I said, raising my voice to an appropriate register. "Is Rev. Jessup inside?"

The flesh around her eyes crinkled. She regarded me for an instant, then shifted her attention back to her legal pad.

"Yes, but the church is filled to capacity. You can't go in now. A few drops of rain and everyone wants to go inside."

Her irritation at my question was palpable. She wore a plastic badge secured by a metal chain around her neck. It identified her as a member of Jessup's staff. She looked dismissively at me and shook her right wrist. An expensive gold chain jangled against her gold watch.

"Are you a church member?" she asked.

"No. I was invited by Mr. Jessup."

"Press?"

"No. A friend."

"Really." She looked me over and then a gleam of recognition streaked through her eyes.

A drag queen is a woman for all seasons.

"Oh, yes," she said. "I do remember you. Lee Ann Blakely from Idaho?"

"The same."

She extended her hand and I took it lightly making sure to touch her only with the pads of my fingers.

"I'm Janice Carpenter," she said. "Public Relations for the Council. I believe we met in New Orleans."

"We certainly did."

Applause burst from inside the church and for an instant I heard the amplified voice of Rodney Jessup, the lilting tone and timbre the same as the night before.

"Excuse me," Janice said. "I have to go inside to complete press arrangements...make sure people are happy. I've got reporters out here who want seats, but if I can find a place I'll come get you."

"Thank you so much," I said, and then smiled as broadly as I could. I peered inside as Janice pulled open the door. The stark interior was lit with the intensity of July Fourth fireworks. Rodney Jessup, arms raised into an exultant V, basked in the adoration and applause of the crowd before him.

A small woman with thick arms and legs waddled up the lawn toward me.

"Have you seen Reverend Jessup?" she cooed. "He's *soooooo* gorgeous and *soooooo* wonderful. I wish he wasn't married."

"He's my kind of man," I said. "Why when we were in New Orleans—" I couldn't go further with the lie.

The woman poked her face closer to mine. "I understand he's very devoted to his wife. Did you hear what happened in New Orleans?"

"Yes."

She was more than willing to go on with her story. "Well, the nerve of that woman. I never did find out who, but some woman from the Midwest made a big pass at Reverend Jessup. He had to fight her off." She jiggled her large arms. "She barged right into his room and threw herself at him. He had to have her escorted from the hotel. Rumors flew all over. Janice—I saw you talking to her—she's in charge of PR, she had to handle it for Reverend Jessup because he's much too busy to put up with that. Imagine, that woman had to be hauled out by hotel security. Janice even wanted to print a story about it in the Council bulletin; but Reverend Jessup being the kind man he is, not wanting to hurt this woman, talked Janice out of it. He's such a dear man. Can you imagine? Such is the price of fame and virtue. Some women have no morals."

"Oh, don't I know."

"Where do you live?" she asked me. "I can't remember, dear."

"Idaho. Spud country. And you? I can't remember either."

"Ohio."

The church door opened as a reporter walked out and the woman pointed a chubby finger inside. "Look! There's Zaleen, from Nebraska. I bet she's the one. Look at her. She always looks as if she's ready to pounce."

Zaleen was unknown to me, but my companion's finger led my eye to an average-looking brunette sitting in a back pew. She didn't look at all the type to force herself on a man, let alone Rodney Jessup.

Janice Carpenter made her way toward the door. There was another blast of applause and cheering, and Janice motioned for me to come inside. I waved "toddles" to the large woman, who frowned as the door closed in her face.

Janice escorted me to an aisle seat in the back pew, apparently the one vacated by the reporter. The combination of lights, muggy air, and squished bodies had turned the church into a living hell. Two small window air conditioners churned at top speed, but hardly dented the inferno inside. I hoped my makeup would hold up.

Rodney Jessup, erect, poised, and confident, worked the microphone and the crowd like a pro. He strode in front of those gathered, his hands cupped in contemplation. One minute he served up the serenity of Buddha, the next the rigid stance of a hell-fire preacher. He lectured his audience, his swooning voters. I admired his style: He mesmerized the crowd despite unbearable conditions.

At one point, after outlining the sacrifices he would have to make to run for President, he extended his hand to his wife, Carol Kingman Jessup, a blonde who sat in the front pew. I could only see the back of her head. "I stand before you today, humbled and honored, on the verge of the creation of a great America. I will lead you in that creation." He walked back to the oak pulpit. When he looked around the sanctuary, I was sure he looked at me; however, I suppose everyone in the church felt the same way. Cameras clicked behind me.

"Today, I have formed a presidential exploratory committee in my bid for the presidency of the United States."

The crowd broke into wild applause amid chants of "We want Rodney." He quieted the crowd with his hands, and then made the usual political pitch for support and money, while outlining all the ills of America. He was better than Elmer Gantry and a lot more dangerous.

He ended by saying, "Thank you for your love and prayers. God bless us. And God bless America!"

Every man, woman, and child stood and cheered. I stood as well because I didn't want to be different—to stand out among the adoring throng. It was revolting to cheer on a man who couldn't care less about me or those like me, but it had to be done for Stephen's sake.

Rodney clasped his hands over his head in a victory sign, then stepped down from the pulpit and shook hands with the men and women in the front pews. Others moved forward to greet him. Janice Carpenter skirted around him like a hovering bee, directing reporters and photographers. Rodney kissed all the children amid flashbulbs and video cameras. He began his walk up the center aisle, shaking hands all the way. Lightning flashed through the windows and the church lights flickered.

He walked toward me without a hint of recognition. He extended his hand and as he did so, I stuck my right leg in front of him.

He stumbled, arms splayed, and then fell with a thud on the red carpet.

Janice, following a few feet behind, screamed. Others joined in the chorus of gasps and exclamations.

I bent down quickly and whispered in his ear, "I need to talk to you about Stephen Cross. Alone."

He looked up at me with wild eyes; a disbelieving horror spread across his face.

"Get back!" Janice yelled and tugged at my shoulder. I felt her hand go limp against the muscles of my back.

I helped Rodney from the floor and smiled at Janice. She stared back, her eyes blazing.

"Are you hurt, Rodney?" Janice asked.

Rodney rubbed his reddened palms gingerly. "No. Just a little carpet burn."

"Let me help you," I said and then hooked my arm through his.

"Get away," Janice hissed.

"It's all right," Rodney told Janice as he smoothed his rumpled suit. "Let Miss...uh, walk with me for a moment. Gather everyone in the Fellowship Room."

Rodney pointed to the back of the church and a deserted office. "So, Miss...."

"Lee Ann Blakely."

"Yes, we've met."

"So I've heard." I lowered my voice. "Stephen Cross has disappeared."

We stepped into the office and Rodney closed the door.

"What has this got to do with me? Mr. Harper isn't it?"

"The very one. Right now, I'm in a lot of trouble and I don't want more. All I want is the truth. Is it a coincidence you were at the hotel last night?"

"Like I told you, Mr. Harper, you are always welcome. Extremism isn't needed. I have obligations to fulfill right now. The press and the crowd are hungry and so am I. I don't think you want me to disappoint. They might get suspicious."

The last thing I wanted was a troop of reporters on my tail, so I agreed with Rodney's point.

"Have something to eat," he said. "We can talk after the fellowship dinner. I'll make sure the church is cleared."

"Please make certain you're a man of your word. I can make your life hell."

I opened the door and said, "Thank you, Reverend Jessup," in my feminine register. A group of the faithful, including the large woman I had met outside, had followed us down the hall.

"Reverend Jessup fell, Lee Ann," the chubby woman said to me as I passed her.

"Yes, honey, he certainly did."

* * *

I was dying for a cigarette an hour after dinner. The thunderstorm had passed, but the air was as soupy as wet cotton. Low gray clouds streamed overhead, pushed by a strong southwest wind. The church stood like a mausoleum, its façade illuminated by spotlights.

Dinner had been an experience to say the least. I felt like Daniel in the lions' den. A man named Lester gave a quick blessing in front of tables piled high with food and Rodney took his place at the head of the line. I made my way through the wholesome, shiny crowd, talking to no one and retired with my plate to one of the brown metal folding chairs lined against the wall. I stuffed myself until I couldn't eat another bite and then slipped from the room.

Only a few cars remained on the lot when I decided to return to the church. I passed a black luxury limousine with a driver. The car, I assumed, was for Rodney and his entourage. I pulled on the church's front door, but it was locked. I walked down the wet flagstone path to a red side door. It opened into a small, dark kitchen.

My heels clicked lightly on the linoleum floor until I found my way into the carpeted sanctuary. The outside spotlights illuminated the stained glass windows and threw misty colors on the beamed ceiling. Christ. Christ blessing the children. Christ blessing the animals. Christ on the Sea of Galilee. Christ in the Garden.

I saw him, sitting in the front pew, staring at the window— Christ on the Cross—behind the altar. As I approached, he glanced at me casually, as if expecting my company and his face seemed as blank as a man without God, expressionless and robotic, a face lacking joy and redemption. He lowered his head and prayed; he curled a leather-bound Bible between his hands. I sat beside him and waited for him to raise his head.

After a time, he began to speak but didn't look at me. "I love my life, Mr. Harper. I have a wonderful wife and two children. This business with Stephen Cross is insanity."

His voice was like a wave, crashing and receding, at once strong and weak.

"I *knew* that summer day north of Waynesboro on the Appalachian Trail. Have you been to Virginia, Mr. Harper?"

"I passed through in a car once."

He turned and I could not look away from his eyes, as glazed as a porcelain doll. He slumped against the pew, drained. The lapels of his blue suit ballooned in front of him.

"It's beautiful," he continued. "I grew up there, but I knew, as sure as I'm here, that day in the shady woods, ripe with the smell of water and moss, that my destiny was chosen. The world beckoned. I was jolted by a rapture that shook me for hours. I lost myself. I didn't know where I was. I prayed for the forgiveness of my sins, as I prayed for the forgiveness of the sins of all people. When the rapture fell away, an exhilarating, powerful charge remained. In the quaint term, Mr. Harper, I received 'the call'. I understood the power. The Lord had spoken to me. I felt invincible, Mr. Harper, and, most of the time I still do. That's why I'm running for President. Invincibility—the invincibility of God's will."

"Very nice," I said, "but it doesn't get me any closer to the answer I want. Where's Stephen?"

He chuckled and little flecks of light danced in his eyes. "I don't know, but Stephen Cross is not the issue. Neither you, nor Stephen Cross, not even the Rev. Rodney H. Jessup, Founder of the Council for Religious Advancement, matters. What matters is God's will be done." He pointed at me and laughed. "I sit here, giving you my time. *You.* Dressed as a woman."

"Why are you talking to me?"

"Because I want this rumor to go no further. Because I also want to know how far it's gone."

"A few people. It doesn't have to go any further."

"My wife suffered two miscarriages within the first three years of our marriage. Do you know how beautiful she is? She erased the years I wasted; erased the damnable mistakes of my life. She saved me."

It was my turn to chuckle. "I thought God saved you."

"Always the cynic, Mr. Harper. Carol saved my life. God saved my soul. When we adopted Ruthie and John four years ago, we did so out of Christian duty, not biological need. They were orphaned in a South Carolina fire, leaving them with no surviving relatives. This thick-jawed ass of a reporter from New York called me a 'grandstanding profiteer of misfortune.' But I held firm, Mr. Harper. Decency triumphed. They are after me. All of them. Waiting for one mistake, one error to bring me down. Even a lie."

"It wasn't a lie, Rodney."

"Don't you dare judge me," he said, his voice veering toward anger. "Do you think this man, Stephen Cross, any man, could change the way I feel about my wife? He will not be made a martyr at my expense."

"You betrayed Stephen."

He folded his hands around the Bible, shut his eyes, and prayed. "You gave me the means to fight this, Lord. You wanted me to fight this evil. Don't punish me now. I did what you wanted."

"Look at me, Rodney. Am I evil because I want to save his life?"

He turned and stared; the glaze was gone from the pupils. The irises crackled. "I love your holy spirit, Mr. Harper, but your soul will be lost unless you give yourself to the Lord, our Savior. Your actions will doom you. There is no evil in repentance and conversion to God. What power there is in God's love, Mr. Harper."

He leaned toward me, and, for an instant, I thought he might kiss me on my left cheek, but the church lights came up with a harrowing brilliance. Carol Kingman Jessup and Janice Carpenter soon appeared in front of us.

"Time to go, Rodney," Carol said. The ice oozed from her eyes.

"And you, too, Lee Ann," Janice said. She lifted her notepad and smirked. "You fooled us for a while, but you're an open book with the police. You've got a great past: small-time drug dealer, hustler. Now you're wanted in Boston for escape from a police officer and suspicion of murder. Reverend Jessup would only have to say the word and you'd be in jail."

"Let him go, Janice," Rodney said without looking away from Christ. "We must learn to forgive."

I knew when to make a propitious exit.

"He's in love with a friend," Rodney said to the women.

I took off my wig and let my hair fall free. Carol shook her head in disgust.

"Maybe you're telling the truth," I said to Rodney.

"I am," he said and finally looked my way. "I wanted to save us all from this disaster. We would never have known about this supposed announcement if it hadn't been for that Boston police officer."

"What was his name, Janice?" Rodney asked.

"Detective Spinetti. I just got off the phone with him."

Rodney smiled at me.

THIRTEEN

HIS SECOND FATHER HAD TAUGHT HIM WELL.

"All you do, you do for me. I am your source, your supply," Jack intones over the man.

He looks at his captive, silent, spread-eagled on the bed. He's given him no food, only a little water. The man grows weaker tonight. The rain sounds like hammers on the roof. He wants his second father to be proud, to see that he understood his training; that he has served well.

"What'd you boys see?"

"Nothing."

"Nothing? Good."

"The perverts almost ganged up on us," Jack said. The others gathered around the campfire and snickered. "We followed orders, but we didn't see anything."

They had burned the house, set it on fire with the perverts inside.

The second father's face, glowing from the fire, grew serious.

"The less you know, the better. You followed command. Discipline teaches you to look and then look away. These days you have to know outsiders as well as you know your own dick."

The second father looked at the campers, pickups and RVs spread out across the dark prairie. Two hundred believers gathered at a private ranch in Oklahoma. Light and shadow flashed from the campfires. Distant farm lights twinkled on the horizon. The wind swept the clouds free of the moon and opened a deep, black sky.

"Yahweh will guide us," the father said and then thrust his head back and studied the stars.

The father loves Yahweh, loves to talk about the benevolence of Yahweh. The new Christian. The movement.

"You will love Yahweh as you love me."

It's a small oath that will bind them until death.

Stephen Cross—the man he wants dead. The man who blasphemed, made a mockery of all that was good and true through his writing.

Could his second father be any more proud of him than when he presents Stephen Cross?

Half a million dollars. Jack doesn't know how the threat started. Maybe his second father offered the money—he talks about cleansing the world of the unclean, the enemy. What difference would one less homosexual in the world make anyway?

Jack's throat tightens. What if his new father is not proud of him? What if he rejects him? But he has to believe this father will not abandon him like his biological father. Jack was, after all, a top performer, a quick learner, able to supervise the digging of plumbing lines as aptly as leading new members in drills. He was grateful to have food, clothing, a new girlfriend, all the privileges bestowed upon him.

Let his new father come. Let him gaze upon the man he has

133

captured. How could he not be proud? His second father loves everything about him: the military cut of his hair, the light brown eyes, the tiny red scar below the left ear, and the few chickenpox scars on his face. Sometimes Jack takes off his clothes, stands naked before the mirror, and stares at his body, searching for perfection. He is a little too short, yet muscled enough. But there are those who admire his youth and the potential it offers.

"Talk to me," he orders the man on the bed. The man smells; his sweat soaks the sheets. "Pay attention to me."

The man stirs, but not to Jack's liking.

The voice comes thin, like a rasp, "Please, let me go."

He stares at the man as he has done all day. He hasn't moved except to go to the bathroom with him.

"We have killed an enemy, sir," he said to his second father. "Perverts." His voice was calm, matter-of-fact. The drills had helped him maintain his composure. They had spent the day training.

"Why did you kill?" his father asked.

"They were a threat. They existed."

"Who are the threats?"

"Perverts, Jews, Negroes, racial mixtures."

"Why these?"

"Training. They were the ones we were after."

"You know that for sure?"

"Yes, sir."

"You did this of your own free will?"

"Yes, sir."

He leans forward and touches the man's foot. He strokes the black hair around the ankle.

"If you love me, love me like your son," he told his second father. "Talk to me about perversion—the filth spread by the homosexuals. I'll absorb these facts and I'll act. No one has to tell me what to do. 'Use your head,' you say. Intelligence. Discipline. Training. I act for the good of the organization and the future of America."

"Love me as you would love no other," the father said. They were gathered in a large barn inside the Oklahoma campground. It was mid-afternoon and everyone was relaxed. The air was filled with the warm smells of animals and hay. Hazy streaks of sunlight slanted through the cracks in the roof.

"Love me," the father repeated. "Know their sins, yet destroy the abomination."

"Love me and no other," the father said.

* * *

The memory floats back to him, the salty taste on his tongue. His younger brother shivering in bed; the day his brother died.

He slides his hands up from the ankles, pushes Stephen's inner thighs apart. Why wait?

"God, no," Stephen whimpers. "Don't."

"Love me," Jack says and climbs up on him, matches his body to his and molds himself to the skin underneath.

The man clinches his buttocks tight. "Christ, no."

Jack rubs against him; Stephen's chest hair scratches against his smooth flesh.

Engorged. *Know their sin, yet destroy them.*

He pulls away. He will keep his prize yet another day.

Jack wakes up near him. The morning sun filters through the pines; the air is cool and dry.

He unties the bindings from the feet, lifts the bound wrists over the pole attached to the bed, but makes sure the rope around Stephen's waist is secure.

Jack watches as Stephen sits on the toilet. He allows him to shower. One more day of training.

Jack dresses and prepares a breakfast of runny scrambled eggs and soggy bacon for Stephen. He spoons the food onto a white paper plate. Stephen scoops up the food with his fingers, shoving it eagerly into his mouth. In mid-bite he spits the eggs on the floor.

"Are you fucking crazy?" Jack glares at him.

"They're poisoned," Stephen says.

"It's garlic. Garlic from the earth gives you power. If you think breakfast is going to kill you, I'll throw it away."

Stephen shakes his head, bends over, and scoops little bits of egg off the floor onto his fingers.

"Do you know anything about hunting?" Jack asks.

Stephen nods. "I did some target practice with my father in Kansas. I never shot anything."

Jack reaches across the table, fingers the leather strap around Stephen's neck, and fondles the round metal. "That's a bullet."

"Yes."

"You sure you haven't killed anything?"

Stephen nods his head.

"Too bad."

Stephen stops chewing. "What do you mean?"

"Not much time left for us." Jack looks out the window into the blackish depths of the forest and then rises from the table. He unlocks an oak chest on the other side of the room and takes his .22 rifle out of its case, secures the shoulder strap and hitches the weapon over his left arm. He rummages in the chest and also withdraws a leather collar—studded metal with attached D rings—which he snaps around Stephen's neck and secures with a small lock. Jack attaches a chain to one of the D rings and jerks Stephen's neck with a rough tug.

"Here boy," Jack says and then laughs. "Time to go for our walk." He pulls Stephen from the table through the cabin, out the door, and into the cool morning shade. A pine-scented breeze washes over his body. He pulls Stephen along, as he walks toward the hazy green wall of trees ahead.

"I saw a picture once in *Life Magazine*," he says to Stephen. "This town in Ohio held a fox hunt—and when I say the town, I mean the whole town. They all got behind it. Not just the men—this was men, women, and children. The whole damn town loved to kill."

Jack pulls him faster through the forest. The pine branches brush against Jack's clothes, but scratch Stephen.

"They'd hunt in May. The men would have a drink or two before breakfast, then they'd crowd into their cars and drive out in the country. All the men, women, and children would form a big circle in the woods, and one of the men—the chosen one—carried a box into the center of a field. At noon, he opened the box and let the fox go."

Stephen stumbles against a rotting stump and yelps in pain. Jack pulls harder on the collar.

"Got to keep running, pervert. You know what happened then? They hunted. The people had clubs, even the kids. They beat the ground with their clubs, slowly closing in on the fox. What do they call a fox?"

"Sly," Stephen answers.

"Sly." Jack laughs. "This fox ain't so sly. He was loose, free, but then those clubs started falling around him. When he heard, maybe felt, the thuds on the ground, he went crazy. He ran in circles, getting ever smaller as the people drew closer. He didn't use his brain. He could have made a break through an opening.

"This poor sucker fox was in the center, snarling and snapping and trying to tear itself to pieces, crazy with fear. The townspeople beat it to death. Even the kids got in some good whacks. Its skin was displayed on a stick in the center of town. Then everybody went home and had lunch. That's when the hunt ended."

Jack leads Stephen past a dark cemetery deep in the woods.

"Is that your plan?" Stephen asks. "Let me go, club me to death and then go home for lunch?"

Jack chuckles. "I thought about it, but I'm not going to. I've thought about that fox for years and how the circle can close in on you." He smiles. The forest is cool under the green canopy. Jack stops and listens to the gentle brush of the wind through the pines and the tumbling rush of a nearby stream.

"Get down," Jack whispers. "Lie flat." He pushes Stephen down into a bed of rust-brown pine needles and settles in beside him being careful to avoid the cuts and welts, rivulets of blood that scar Stephen's body.

At the stream, near a pool, Jack sees a brown-and-white shape drift out of the trees: A three-point buck on his way to drink. He watches the deer, an animal of steady eyes and cautious gait. The noble head, the strength of the flank impress him. This animal can jump six to eight feet straight up with ease.

Jack rises slowly from the needles. He doesn't want the deer to smell or see him and dart away; his chance of hitting a buck in full flight is slim. The animal cocks his head, but keeps his place by the stream. Jack lifts himself higher and straddles Stephen's back.

"Stretch out your arms," Jack whispers. "I'm giving you the rifle." He stifles a laugh. What a game! giving the prisoner the weapon.

"Keep it pointed forward or you're dead." Jack fits his finger through the collar. "I can break your neck. Pull the trigger and kill the deer." He lowers the rifle to Stephen's outstretched hands. The buck turns a cautious eye upstream.

"Do it," Jack says. "It's easy. Imagine the deer's queer."

"Kill it yourself," Stephen says and drops the rifle.

Jack lifts the collar until Stephen's face turns blue and he gasps for air.

The deer, with a startling quickness, leaps over the stream and vanishes into the green thicket.

"Fuck!" Jack releases Stephen, grabs the rifle, and sights through the trees. He hears branches snap, and for an instant he sees the brown-and-white form under the shadows. The rifle cracks, a sharp ping whizzes through the air. The buck jumps and then crashes to the ground.

Jack laughs. "I got the fucker." He is still straddled over Stephen. The prisoner makes a quick thrust upward, knocking Jack off his feet, sending him crashing into a small pine tree. The rifle flies over Jack's head.

Stephen is quick, but his strength is sapped from his ordeal. Jack is faster and is back on his feet in a few seconds. Stephen rises on his haunches but the steel-toed boot catches him in the back, shoving him to the ground in spasms of pain. Jack's boot raises a print on Stephen's back.

"Try that again, motherfucker, and you're dead." Jack retrieves the rifle, pulls Stephen up by the collar, and walks him to the deer. The animal, shot near the heart, is wounded and struggling.

"I have to kill the son-of-a-bitch because you can't do it." He positions the rifle behind the deer's left ear and pulls the trigger. The flesh explodes around the wound. The deer kicks with his legs and then falls silent. Jack strokes the shiny fur and pulls up a spot of blood with his index finger. With the blood, he marks a cross near Stephen's heart.

"Target practice," Jack says.

Jack drags him to the mound. Three crosses rise from the black dirt.

Vacant horror spreads across Stephen's face when he sees the two men strapped to the beams. It is exactly the look Jack wanted.

"You can't bargain with a psycho, Stephen. That's what they call me in the papers. A psychopath. The Combat Zone Killer. Do you know how that hurts? Everybody always called me crazy. I was the 'crazy one' who killed my brother and I didn't even do it." He trembles a little. "You'll listen to me won't you?"

Stephen nods his head.

"You can make it all right?"

"I'll try."

"Just like daddy?"

"Yes."

"Daddy was the one who killed him. I didn't, but I took it because I had to. I was so little and scared. And then I believed I did it because everybody told me so. I had no choice."

Stephen stares at him and says, "But you have a choice now. You don't have to kill. Someone will...I'll help you."

Jack puts his index finger across Stephen's mouth and then runs his fingers over the dry lips and the stubble on his cheeks. "No one can help me know. They'll just put me away, like they did when they took me away from home. I'd never been so alone—like there was nobody else on earth. I couldn't take it. All I wanted was for him to love me." He points toward the mound. "But I don't want love like yours. It's sick and diseased."

"It's just love."

"No, Carl says it's not that way. It's a sin. The only love is between a man and a woman, just like it says in the Bible. That's the way it should be. No room for adulterers or perverts."

"Who's Carl?" Stephen asks.

"My second father. The man who saved me, who taught me."

"Can I talk to Carl?"

Jack laughs. "If I had given you to Carl, you would have been dead a long time ago. But I don't see Carl anymore. He lives over the mountain, at the compound. I did everything for him, but there was trouble and now he won't see me. He says he doesn't know me. I killed that queer in the theater in Boston and that married queer at the rest stop. And then I killed Clay."

"Clay Krieger?"

"Shit, you knew him?"

"A friend told me about him."

"Clay got around. That was hard; he was like a brother to me. But he pissed on me. The asshole fucked my woman. Carl got mad and threw us both out. I wanted to kill Clay because he separated me from my father. Once I heard about the reward, you were easy. All I had to do was read those queer papers. I saw you were going to be at the hotel. But, Clay, I happened to run into him in the Zone the night before I got you. So, the count keeps going up and when Carl finds out what I've done, he'll take me back in a second."

"You're going to get rich by killing me?"

"I haven't seen the money, but I know it's there. Everybody at the compound knew before I left. If anybody can get a half-million, it'd be Carl. He's connected."

"I can raise the money," Stephen says.

"I don't want *your* money. You're a pervert. What does Carl say? Oh, yeah, 'an abomination.'" He points toward the crosses. "I got these two coming out of a bar, arms around each other, just after closing. Didn't know what hit them. Hardly had Clay's blood off my knife. They're not dead yet, but they will be after you kill them."

Stephen shakes his head.

"There are two possibilities—you can watch me carve them up like stuck pigs, or you can kill them. What would a real man do?" Jack laughs loud and hard. "Shit. I've been reading too many books."

A low moan drifts from one of the crosses. Jack drags Stephen closer. The dappled sunlight plays over the men nailed and strapped to the beams and Jack smiles because life is good.

CHAPTER FOURTEEN

How weary, stale, flat, and unprofitable
Seem to me all the uses of this world!

HOW TRUE THE WORDS THE PRINCE OF DENMARK spoke. How sad this morning at the cheap motel in Manchester. I have no tower in which to take refuge, no father's ghost, no mother's shoulder to catch my tears.

I struggled to get out of bed. I took a warm shower, hoping to wash away my lethargy. The past day had left me anxious and harboring an uncomfortable feeling of depression—like a brick in my head. I looked in the bathroom mirror: My eyes were dark and my face was as sallow as a drunk after a three-day binge. The man in my dream, Stephen, was pulling me deeper into the vat despite every push and shove against him.

For all my gloom, nature had provided a blazing sun in a spotless blue sky. It was the kind of sun—a ball of white-hot, piercing rays—that would make you blind if you looked at it long enough. The bright clarity of the day was in sharp contrast to my hazy confusion.

I thought of calling John Dresser to get an update on Stephen, but decided against it fearing the phone might be tapped. By now, every cop in New Hampshire knew I was in the Manchester area thanks to Chris, but there was no reason to take chances. John probably wanted nothing to do with me anyway. In my gut, I felt Stephen was alive, a supposition grounded only in intuition. I flipped through the television news channels, but neither Stephen nor I were mentioned. The only other lead I could check out that seemed probable was the Aryan America compound near Warren. Perhaps they might be holding Stephen to the tune of a half a million dollars.

There was another troubling issue for me. Why had Chris Spinetti called Rodney Jessup to tell him of Stephen's intended "outing?" Why the favor? Those questions ran through my head all night. Chris might have an APB out on me for murder, but he had to know that if I found out that underhanded trick of his, I would be one pissed-as-hell queer with some questions of my own.

The same disinterested gray-haired man who had checked me in, checked me out around 9:45 a.m. "Thank you, Mr. Swerdloe," he said. "Enjoy your stay in New Hampshire."

I blinked, but recovered. I'd forgotten my alias—a stupid mistake.

I made one stop at the Mall of New Hampshire. I swigged down a cup of strong black coffee and ate a strawberry jelly donut. Nutrition was not foremost on my mind. I bought a Red Sox baseball cap from a man operating a hat business from a cart. I wanted to look as straight as possible when I got to Warren. I could hide my hair as easily under an "I've got balls" cap as I could my GlamourTress wig.

It was risky, but in order to save time, I drove the Cavalier up I-93 until I got to Route 25 near Plymouth. I kept looking over my shoulder. Near Franklin, an olive-colored state patrol car whizzed past me at a high rate of speed, intent on some other business. I froze when I saw the fast-moving vehicle in the rear-view mirror, but the trooper never gave me a look.

The closer I got to Warren, the greener and more mountainous the land became along the spine of the Appalachian Trail, nearly a thousand miles from Rodney Jessup's conversion. What had I expected from him last night at the church? A clue? A confession? Remorse? Whatever Rodney Jessup knew was of no help to me now.

The shallow, wooded peaks of the White Mountains surrounded me. Warren was as charming as a happy New England post-card. On any other day, I could have been content being a tourist basking in the warm sunshine and cool mountain air. I parked the car at Land's General Store on the main highway, an establishment straight out of *Green Acres*, complete with a screened-in porch and a creaky plank floor. The store smelled delicious: A sweet mixture of baked breads, coffee, and chocolate all wrapped in the milky glacial air of an open ice cream freezer. A gray tiger cat swished its tail at me and possessively held its place on the polished oak check-out counter. Behind it, a pretty, trim woman in blue jeans and a white sweatshirt gave me a smile. She was marking items off on an inventory list. She pushed back her brown hair with her hands and deftly placed her pen behind her right ear.

"Hello. What can I do for you?" Her voice was pleasant, unaffected.

I picked up a package of M&Ms. "I'd like these, and, if you have it, a turkey sandwich on light rye with mustard, lettuce and tomato."

"Sure." She turned and yelled, "David" to the back of the store.

A man wearing a blood-spotted chef's apron over his work shirt and jeans, stepped out of the back room and stood behind the meat counter. His eyes were pleasant and eager and his rugged face was set off by a full black beard. The woman repeated my sandwich instructions.

"Anything else?" she asked.

"Maybe a Coke."

I twirled a quarter on the slick counter.

"Drinks are in the cooler," she said and pointed across the room.

"A question," I said. "Can you tell me how to get to Aryan America?"

She stared at me. David stopped slicing the turkey.

"You from the city?" she asked.

I nodded. "Boston. Looking for a friend."

She smiled, the briefest glimpse of teeth appeared between her lips. "I don't think any friend of yours would be with Carl Roy. Not many gay men around here, let alone *out* around here."

I looked down at my shirt and jeans. "Did I forget to take my gay sign off?" I asked, disgruntled I couldn't pull off the straight charade. "The Red Sox cap didn't help?"

The woman laughed and David said, "Ann's got a sense. Her brother's gay."

"We don't make a big deal of it," Ann said. "We're from Hartford. We came to Warren to get away from the city, the crime, all the metro stuff. Our dream was to run a country store. So, we ended up with Carl Roy instead."

"Guess I should brush up on butch."

"Carl's not half bad—at least to us," Ann said. "He comes in all the time. Acts like any other customer. We say, 'Hello, Carl. How's the family?' and he'll say 'Just fine, how's yours?' and off he goes. That's about as deep as it gets. We're glad we don't have a pickle barrel, although we've been thinking about getting one."

"We've never seen a bad side of Carl," David said.

"What's he like?" I asked.

"Squat, like a bulldog," David explained. "Bulldogs are really gentle, you know."

"Carl may look like a bulldog," I said, "but from what I hear he's more like a pit viper."

"Thinning red hair," David continued, ignoring my comment. "Could have been a middle-weight boxer."

"Sounds formidable."

Ann rang up my order. "Most people in town tolerate him. 'Live free or die,' you know. He keeps his nose clean; never gets into trouble. Most folks don't care what he does as long as he doesn't bother them. On the other hand, there are little pockets of Carl's believers spread throughout the mountains. He gets mail from all over the world. We hear rumors, but we keep out of it. He can believe what he wants."

"How do I find him?"

Ann narrowed her eyes. David stepped around the counter and handed me my sandwich. He was lumberjack material.

"You sure you want directions?" she asked.

"A close friend of mine may be staying with Carl. I need to find him."

"Okay," she said, not hiding her disbelief at my story, "but you didn't hear it from us. I don't want Carl to think we're sending him uninvited guests. What's your name?"

"Des."

"Well, Des, good luck. I hope you find your friend."

She extended her hand. I grasped it and she shook mine warmly.

The Lands told me to look for a blockade entrance about six miles north of Warren on Route 118. Mt. Cushman would be clearly visible on my right when I got near the road. They said the property was ringed by a high fence, some of it electrified, and the house, although they had never been there, was a least a half-mile back from the road.

There was little traffic along the way. A few puffy white clouds dotted the sky above the peaks. I slowed the Cavalier when the gentle slope of a higher mountain came into view through the passenger windows. I drove a quarter mile more and stopped near an iron gate with "No Trespassing" and "Private Property" signs posted on it. An intercom box, inscribed "C. Roy" stood to the right of the gate. I'd found Aryan America.

No matter my fondness for drama, I didn't want to make an entrance through the front gate. I turned the car around and followed the fence until it ended at a lumber road that cut into the woods. The Cavalier rumbled over the potholes and exposed rocks. I parked the car when the road fell away to narrow tracks.

The wind brushed through the tamarack and tall pines, on land studded with quaking aspen, mountain birch and striped maples, all verdant and serene as if locked in place for eternity. The light, quivering and diffuse, transformed the forest into an infinite sea of green.

I opened the trunk and loaded the .357. I had neglected to pack my holster and I dreaded the cold metal between my stomach and jeans. I reconsidered taking the gun. Unarmed, my chances of being taken as an innocent hiker—someone lost in the woods— were better. I really knew nothing about how Aryan America operated. I might discover a fortress or a farmhouse; a militia or a few disgruntled farmers. I closed the trunk, concerned about the safety of my possessions, and hiked into the woods toward Aryan America.

The forest floor was a landmine of noises. Small branches cracked under my feet and every step brought up the crackle of dead leaves. Every crunch gave away my location, but whenever I stopped, I saw nothing but trees and heard nothing but the tremble of the wind.

After about 15 minutes, I came to a wire fence. There was no attempt to hide the electrification. A few white knobs, insulators, were wired on a supporting post. I pitched a downed branch onto one of the wires, but the limb bounced back without a hiss or a puff. A frosting of barbed wire made the fence at least five feet tall, high enough I couldn't jump it. I walked parallel until I came to a large rock outcropping that split the fence. This is too easy, I thought. I was right. I could climb the outcrop and avoid the fence. The only drawback was the 15-foot deep ravine I would drop into unless I made a clean jump across the chasm. If I executed the jump correctly, I would land between the trunks of two gnarled trees. If not, I would end up in a hole with a broken skull. Or worse.

I stopped to piss.

I sat on the outcropping and felt the cold and mossy damp of the rock sink into my jeans. The woods breathed around me.

"There's a lot of money to be made here," I said to the forest. I pulled the Marlboros from my jeans. "Half a million dollars. A nice sum."

I imagined what I could do with the money. I could retire to Costa Rica and live like a king for years. I could have Costa Rican men day and night. I could live in Mexico and open a leather shop. I could have Mexican men day and night. I could live on a secluded Caribbean island and lie naked in the sun. I could have island men day and night. I could get out of this miserable life I had been stuck in forever.

Or I could forget all this, turn back and return to the stolen car. Maybe start life over.

To proceed further, to make this jump across the chasm to Aryan America would be an admission, a break in the DNA of my life. If I jumped, I might as well admit that Stephen was more to me than a friend. He was the lover I always wanted; a man I respected and admired, and a man who was so devoted to John Dresser that my fantasy was doomed to wallow in the self pity of my heart. Yet, sitting here, I realized that when I came to his aid in the horrifying stillness outside the bar two years ago, I saved more than Stephen's life.

I saved my own.

I could thank him now by taking the leap. He might thank me for it later.

I crushed the cigarette into the green moss.

The lyrics to *People* ran through my head. I sang and laughed in the woods.

Then I leaped off the rock.

CHAPTER FIFTEEN

TWO MEN PLEAD WITH VOICES DIMINISHED BY PAIN.
Three crosses. The middle one on the zenith of the mound empty.

Jack locks the abomination to a tree, captive like a country dog. He sits and then points and laughs. "They're beautiful, aren't they, like some fucking Renaissance painting."

Ropes bind their wrists and feet to the wood. Their skin bleeds rust from their palms and ankles, the limbs swollen, distended, and blue. Their mouths jabber little words Jack can't hear.

"Got glue in your mouth?" Jack taunts.

"Asshole." The word comes from behind.

He points the rifle at Stephen. "Shut up and watch."

He goes to the dark, long-haired man on the left and swivels the head on the wood. The man tenses and little bubbles of saliva froth on his lips.

"Don't touch him," the other says.

He leaves the first and turns to the man on the right with the close-cropped brown hair. He stands beside him and runs his hands over the hairy abdomen, down the torso to the cleft in the legs and lifts the drooping penis.

"This is what causes all our pain," Jack says. "So we get rid of it." He draws a knife from his right pocket and flips it open. He stretches the penis taut until the man screams and bucks on the cross. Jack raises the knife.

"Let them go. You wanted me." The voice behind him. Stephen strains against the collar and pushes his feet into the dirt. The chain holds against the tree.

"You are so kind, so noble...but think again."

Jack raises the knife and cuts a tuft of hair from the man's chest. He walks to Stephen and sprinkles it over him. Stephen is breaking, Jack thinks.

In a second, Jack is at the cross, flashing the knife, carving a swastika into the rigid leg of the long-haired man. The blood forms a runny square from the wound. They are both screaming now and he must shut them up. Jack smashes the rifle butt into their throats, one then the other. The men choke and gag and their heads loll on the crosses. Then he is in Stephen's face, shouting, "You think I won't do it? You think I won't kill them? I have nothing to lose."

The years evaporate. The rage. His brother's blood. A red bomb explodes in his head and he is filled with a prickly numbness like a million little pins pushing from the inside to get out through his skin. "They're dead. Fucking teach you to be queers!"

He draws in violent breaths and clutches his head, as if to seek asylum from the demons that plague him. "Go away! Leave me alone!"

The footsteps come closer. The door opens. *I'll teach you, you little faggots!*

He stumbles to the mound and buries his face against the black earth, the rifle at his side.

* * *

When he opens his eyes, the sun is lower, the air cooler.

Jack jerks his head. His prisoner curls against the rough bark of a pine. He looks at the men on the crosses and believes they are dead.

"Money for *your* hide," he shouts to Stephen. "Carl will be proud."

Stephen is silent against the tree.

"Did you hear me? Carl will be proud!"

His prisoner is hunkering, fetal.

He brushes the dirt from his face and walks to Stephen. He bends to touch him with a brush of his fingers against the shoulder.

The prisoner pulls away violently.

"He'd better be damn proud of me," Jack says, "after what I've done for him. I've done all I can to make it up to him. I've done my duty." Jack's insides shake. He wonders what will happen if he can't talk with Carl—if he rejects him as a son—can't bear to look upon him, can't stand the sound of his voice. Rejection and loneliness are far worse than hate. He unlocks the chain from the tree and pulls it tight against Stephen's neck. Stephen rolls on his back.

Fury dives into Jack's hands and he shakes the chain until it snaps like a whip. *Stupid queer, stupid faggot.* Jack looks into Stephen's bloody eye sockets and tries to scrape the pine needles from the tissue. The blank red eyes stare at him.

Stephen howls in wolfish laughter. "Let me have the rifle now," he taunts.

Jack pulls Stephen to his feet and presses him flat against his body. He forces Stephen's right hand to the trigger, aims the rifle and squeezes Stephen's finger.

One shot. Cartridge ejected. Reload. A second shot. Soft thwacks into flesh. A moan drifts across the clearing. From the trees?

Stephen wrenches the rifle away, whirls, and pulls the trigger. It clicks.

"No bullet in the chamber, pervert."

Stephen swings it in a wide circle, but doesn't hit Jack. The stock whizzes past him in the air.

Jack whips the chain and his prisoner collapses on the ground from the snap. The rifle falls to earth.

Jack sits, disgusted and out of patience. He spits on Stephen and then tugs on the chain. He will take the prisoner back to the cabin.

Carl will come tonight and life will be easier.

CHAPTER SIXTEEN

DARK.

At first, I thought I was blind.

When vision began to break through the blackness in my throbbing head, I realized I was flat on my back, God knows where.

The last thing I remembered was the ground, brown and rocky, rising up before me between the two trees. My right foot twisted and slipped off a rock as slick as ice. My body tumbled toward an ancient Cedar, whose bark surely had gone through the century without once feeling the touch of pliable human flesh. My breath flew out of me—it felt as if a wrecking ball had smashed into my stomach. The lights went out.

The inhabitants of God Knows Where had blindfolded and restrained me on what felt like a sheet of plywood. My head pounded, my back ached, my right ankle throbbed. As I slowly got my senses back, my skin screamed from cuts and scrapes.

I moved my eyes and saw pinholes of light through the fabric. I managed to make out two distinct male voices among the cacophony of others—one of an older man, another who sounded a generation younger.

"Looks like he's coming to," the younger voice said.

"Don't touch him, Adam," the older man stated in calm certainty. "He's still bleeding."

I sensed someone leaning over me and the dots of light in my blindfold went dark.

Cold water poured over my face. I sputtered and shook my head.

"Yep, he's to," the older man said.

The soggy blindfold came off. I blinked out the water and then stared into the acne-scarred face of a young man pointing a high-caliber automatic at the bridge of my nose.

"Pretty stupid, mister," the youngster said. "Sometimes when you fall you trip a security camera."

"That's enough, Adam," the older man said. "Sit down. We don't know this gentleman."

I turned my head and pain stabbed through my forehead. I stared at the man who sat five feet away from me in a rough wooden chair. Just like David Land had said, he looked like a bulldog off a leash.

"Charmed," I said, and strained to lift my bound arms.

The dog showed his teeth and the smile gave me chills—because of its supreme confidence, not because it was sardonic or scary. "Don't be smart," he said in a voice that sounded like a growl. "You're trespassing. I have every right to have you arrested."

I took mental notes on my current accommodations. I was inside a small one-room cabin, empty except for two chairs and the wooden camping cot to which I was tethered. I was stretched out on a plank, placed on top of the cot. A ratty gray blanket covered my feet. A roll of toilet paper lay next to a blue pail in a corner. A single light bulb over my head illuminated the cabin, but a dim yellow light filtered through a dingy window of opaque glass. A group of stout men poked their heads past the cabin door.

"I was out for a walk," I said. "I'd be more than happy to go my way."

"Don't you know where you are?" Adam asked. He sprawled in the other chair, the silver barrel of the automatic pointed toward the floor.

"Somewhere near Warren. If I can get back to the highway...."

The bulldog continued to show his teeth. "You may not be able to walk because your right ankle may be broken." He rubbed the back of his head with his right hand and I saw a tattoo on the inside of his wrist.

Aryan America.

"Carl, we'll be at the house if you need us," one of the men called out and then shut the door.

"So, who are you?" Carl asked. "The truth. You're not from around here."

Fortunately, I remembered the name I used at the Manchester motel. "Bruce Swerdloe."

"Bruce," Carl said and then laughed. "That's a *queer* name."

Adam joined in the gaiety.

What the hell? Was I still wearing that sign?

"Untie him, Adam."

Adam put the gun on the floor and leaned over me.

"I'm—"

"—Carl Roy," I said.

Carl's eyes narrowed and then he grinned. "So you know me. This is my son, Adam. Wasn't easy carrying you on this half-ass stretcher about a half-mile. We strapped you in so you wouldn't hurt yourself."

Adam lifted the ropes and wound them around his left shoulder. I tried my arms—they worked fine. But when I tried to prop myself up on my elbows, the blood boiled in my head, followed by a sickening lightness which swept over my body. I lay back on the plank and took a few deep breaths. I heard a buzz in the corner. A video camera swiveled over my head and the lens tilted toward my body.

"Candid camera," I said.

"Maybe America's funniest videos," Adam countered.

Carl clasped his fingers together and rotated his thumbs in a slow-moving circle. "Maybe if you two comedians would relax for a minute, I could get to the bottom of this. It's a bit unusual for a man to be hiking in the woods around here—no gear, no identification, a Red Sox cap, not exactly on the trail—especially if he knows Carl Roy."

The lepidopterist story wasn't going to fly. "We think alike," I said.

Carl snickered. "You're a smart man—maybe too smart – why would you say something stupid like that? Everybody thinks they know Carl Roy, but they don't."

"I'm looking for a man—there are half-a-million reasons why."

"You're looking for a man? Bet you've looked for plenty."

"A man you might have been looking for, too. Stephen Cross."

Adam sat quietly, the gun dangling from his right hand. Carl's lips parted and his square white teeth gleamed. The bulldog was about to bite.

"Let me tell you about Carl Roy." His voice was tinged with acid. "I like gardening and fishing. I have a little plot out back of the house – summer flowers now, herbs, vegetables that will grow up here. I have a son, Adam, who means the world to me— he's the reason I believe what I do. I don't consider myself polit-ical—just realistic. I want a country that's not going to push him around, rob him at every turn, take away his God-given rights. Look at this country and you'll see a nation of soulless lambs ripe for the slaughter.

"Just give the government time and it'll hang itself. A few

things have made it easier for me. Stupid liberals. The Supreme Court. The ATF. Waco. Oklahoma City. People take me seriously now. Their little world is crashing around them. I don't have to do anything. The fact that *we* exist sets events in motion. So, I don't have much to do now, *Bruce*, except not get into trouble. There's no reason for me to be concerned with this man you're looking for."

I swung my legs off the board and raised my body. The blood drained from my head and a wave of nausea swept over me. I leaned against the rough wall of the cabin. After a few moments, I managed to say, "Funny...Rodney Jessup has the same opinion."

Carl glared at me. "You're in deep shit, aren't you Bruce."

I shrugged.

"President." Carl spit out the word. "Bullshit. He's no better than the rest of them—Democrats, Republicans – I don't care if they're Socialists or Communists. Jessup tells the lambs what they want to hear. He promises something for nothing and they believe it – as long as they aren't affected – as long as their way of life is guaranteed. If the lambs want a guarantee send them to Sears. Jessup believes in politics. I believe in power.

"History is my teacher. Any preacher can pound the pulpit, maybe even get enough momentum going to change some laws in backwater towns, rural states, but all that goes nowhere. Not so with power. Jessup can scream from here to Seattle and still not see himself in power. I don't have to *advocate* anything. I only have to offer safety and belonging to those who have none, the disenfranchised, the alienated. Never underestimate the powerful need to belong. Hitler understood it when he recruited his National Socialists. The first to sign up are those crushed by the government, those who are scratching on the coffin lid of their buried lives."

Carl closed his small, round eyes and leaned back in the chair. "It's too hot to sit here. What should I do with you?"

I put some pressure on my right foot. My ankle screamed.

"It would be easy enough to kill you," Carl said. "Shot while trespassing. Shot while attacking my son. What do you think, Adam?"

Adam stretched out his gangly arm, bone covered by thin flesh, and pointed the barrel toward my chest.

"Where can I find Hugh?" I blurted out, not ready to die at the hands of a 16-year-old.

Carl's eyes flashed. He motioned for Adam to lower the gun. "I don't know anyone by that name."

"I think you do. Clay Krieger told me about Hugh."

A spark of recognition bounced across his face, then a hiss snaked out of his mouth, like the breath off a devil's tongue. "You're the one." He chuckled. "Adam, the answer to our prayers has been cast into our arms. The killer has been delivered to us."

"I didn't kill Clay," I said.

"*Delivered to us.* We have work to do."

Before I could move, they were out the door. I heard the scrape of wood being fitted against wood.

* * *

There is so hot a summer in my bosom,
That all my bowels crumple up to dust:
I am a scribbled form, drawn with a pen
Upon a parchment, and against this fire
Do I shrink up.

—King John

The yellow light fluttered against the window like a swallowtail's wings. Yellow and black, light and dark. It was unlikely I could escape the cabin, but I'd be damned if I didn't try. I massaged my ankle, rose from the cot, and put my full weight on my feet. My right leg nearly gave way in pain, but with perseverance I hobbled around the room. The video camera whirred over my head. My captors were paying close attention to me.

I pointed to the blue pale in the corner, hoping that someone would understand my message—I had to go to the bathroom, this lovely little bucket being my only means of processing elimination. I pulled the cot closer to the camera, stood on it, and wrapped toilet paper over the camera lens. I probably had about three minutes to make a quick inspection of the cabin before my privacy would be interrupted.

I shoved the door; it didn't budge. There was no inside handle. The walls, the floor, the ceiling all appeared sturdy. Upon a closer look, the black vertical lines of bars appeared through the opaque window. Clearly, this cabin was a holding cell.

On cue, there was a rough knocking at the door followed by an expletive in a gruff voice.

"I'm taking a shit," I yelled. I squatted over the blue bucket, and, like a dog, performed.

"Hurry up," Gruffy yelled back.

I wiped and then knocked on the door.

The outside post lifted. A man dressed in a white undershirt and green combat fatigues opened the door.

I handed him the bucket. He looked at its contents and scowled.

"Thanks," I said. "Have a nice day."

Later, Gruffy returned the bucket and ordered me to take the paper off the camera. I complied; my actions were under scrutiny again.

Through the afternoon, anxiety and hunger got the better of me. By the time the light faded through the window, I was strung like a highwire. I looked at my watch; it was around 8 p.m. I moved the plank off the cot. An overpowering tiredness knocked me into a tense sleep in the still, dark cabin.

I hadn't been asleep long when a click in my right ear set every nerve roaring. I stiffened. A cold circle of metal pressed against my temple.

"Someone's finally coming for you, but I've saved them the trouble." I recognized Adam's quivering voice. "You killed Clay."

I spoke calmly, firmly, "Adam, listen to me."

"You're a fairy. You carved up Clay and made it look like one of us did it. I'm going to kill you."

"Carl will be angry."

"Not if the queer attacks *me*—checking on you. The man on the desk wanted a break. I told him I'd watch you. I turned off the monitor. No one can see us."

"Adam, I'm getting up." I rose slowly from the cot.

Adam stepped back. "Go for it, fag."

"Clay was gay," I said. Adam stood, his lean form silhouetted against the window by a porch light. He raised his right arm.

"He was no queer." His voice shook. "I trained with him when I was a kid. I slept in the same room with him. He never tried nothing."

"Clay and I had sex."

A shot exploded in my ears and white-hot heat whizzed past my head. Splinters sprayed across the left side of my face. I dove out of the cot and aimed my head toward Adam's stomach. He crumpled and then toppled over one of the wooden chairs. The gun thudded to floor and I grabbed it.

Adam moaned in the dark. "Oh, fuck, my head."

I punched my left foot hard into his belly and knocked the wind out of him. He gasped for breath. "Don't play with the lights out, you little shit." My right forefinger, itchy, danced on the trigger. "Get up," I screamed at him. "You've tipped off every Nazi in New Hampshire."

I grabbed him by the shirt and dragged him to the door. I kicked it open and we stumbled into the woods. Adam doubled over on his knees. The fading sunlight was orange in the west. To the east, an inky blackness spread through the trees. Ahead, lights from the compound appeared on the horizon. Voices bellowed up from a ridge not more than 500 feet away. I knelt beside Adam and put the gun firmly to his head.

"I want you to remember one name," I said.

Adam's chest heaved and then he sobbed.

"One name," I repeated.

He nodded.

"Dresser. John Dresser. Say it!"

"Dresser," he gasped.

"You're a free man. You owe me. If you ever find out anything about Stephen Cross, call John Dresser in Boston. Understand?"

He nodded again and spit out the name.

The men's voices grew closer, more distinct.

One of the voices taunted me—dared me to stay and fight. My stomach fluttered and a whip of adrenaline drained the pain from my body. I knew the voice—the man coming for me – clear, distinct, from the other side of the ridge. The voice of Chris Spinetti.

Adam cried into the ground.

"It's all right," I said. I touched him on the back, heaved the gun as far as I could into the dark woods and then ran for my life.

SEVENTEEN

"CARL THERE?"

"Who's asking?" Charlie Hollister recognizes the voice on the phone. Charlie's always friendly, a smile for everyone and never forgets a voice or a face. He makes cleaning toilets a good time. Hates dogs, though. Gave a kick to Carl's dog once. Carl nearly went through the roof.

"It's Hugh." No need to be "Jack" with Charlie.

"Hugh. Good to hear from you. Where are you?"

God, Charlie's a joker. He knows where I am. In a dumpy cabin no more than six miles from him. Haven't seen him, though, since the rally in Oklahoma. I might as well be in Alaska.

"Later, Charlie. Just let me talk to Carl."

He can see them, sitting in the kitchen, drinking coffee, playing computer games or sending out messages online, watching the video monitors to the right of the kitchen door. They are ghostly images in stark black-and-white: the spotlighted front gate, the four corners of the compound, the barn and two small cabins deeper in the woods, closer to the north mountains. Charlie,

Randall Kirk, Bill McMurtry, new revolutionaries, gather around the kitchen table. Carl keeps them safe and assures them of their power, their righteousness, their place in the world.

"All hell's breaking loose here," Charlie says. "Not a good time to talk."

"I have to talk to Carl. It's important."

"Maybe he's in the cell. Hold on." The phone goes silent.

How many times had he walked with Carl through the house on their way to the "cell"? That's what Carl jokingly called his office. They'd walk past the conference room, past one of the bedrooms converted to a library, to the video and telecommunications center. There, three computers sat on a 10-foot wooden desk, screens on, sending out the messages through the internet. A large table piled with books and maps filled the center of the room. The north wall was lined with bookshelves which held more maps, books on famous battles, newspapers, histories of Nazi Germany, literature from similar groups from the earth's farthest reaches. At the end of the hall, the house took a sharp right turn. They would stop at a gray metal door, which led to the stone turret. Carl asked him to look away as he punched in the coded lock combination. The lock would click, the door swing open, and the turret lights blaze on. Carl led him up the circular metal staircase, past the narrow slotted openings sealed with iron covers, easily stripped away for defense, to his piece of the castle, his office at the top of the tower. They'd both get an adrenaline kick as they walked past the stockpiled rows of weapons: AK47s, Vz.58 assault rifles, Galil sniping rifles—Carl's favorite. He caressed the rifle like the body of a woman. Past three Barrett Light Fifty sniper rifles purchased for $10,000 before the government stuck its nose into the gun business. The weapons gleamed, oiled and cleaned, resting against the curved stone walls in the only part of the compound kept at a constant 65 degrees and 40 percent humidity. The guns were Carl's babies, part of the arsenal kept by members of Aryan America. Carl made sure the weapons were fired and cleaned regularly by a select few. Hugh had been part of that group—the trusted men who considered it an honor to polish and fire Carl's weapons.

Carl's keys opened the double dead-bolt locks to the cell door. In many respects it was a cell: stone, maybe 18-feet in diameter. It contained only an oak chair, a desk, and a U.S. Army cot for catching a nap. The desk held a bank of video monitors, a pencil sharpener, and a tray for rubber bands and paper clips. With the four directional firing slots covered, the cell was dark and ministerial, the perfect refuge for the leader. Underneath the cot was a wooden weapons chest loaded with handguns: Colt, Beretta, Smith & Wesson, and Glock. The room was gray and dull except for one picture on Carl's desk, a gold-framed snapshot of Adam, when he was about six, sitting beneath a flowering dogwood. Banners and a small Nazi flag were rolled and propped against the wall. Carl had told him that these items were damaging and must be guarded at all costs; they were props for the recruitment of young men. Otherwise, the office was naked except for a small floor safe. No plaques, no photos, no art on the walls.

It took two men and Hugh to carry the safe up the stairs to the cell. One time, Carl opened it when Hugh was in the room. He saw a large paper bag and a couple of sheets of paper Carl called, "my will". Carl dropped a roll of bills into the bag and closed the safe.

The phone clicks. "Carl's not in," Charlie says.

"You sure?"

Charlie sighs. "Look, just between you and me, I'm not even supposed to be talking with you. Carl's fit to be tied right now. I've never seen him so furious. He said you don't exist as far as he's concerned. He even told me not to pick up again. There's too much shit going on right now. So for everybody's sake, Hugh, let it go."

Click.

Overpowering emptiness.

Hugh slams the phone into the cradle and his hands shake. He raises them, trembling, to his eyes and he cries.

* * *

Stephen Cross draws in sleepy breaths through his nose. Duct tape makes a smooth silver line over his mouth.

Hugh watches him from his chair.

Gone. All gone. Useless.

He watches the lazy swell and release of Stephen's ribcage as the dark claws at him. "Going for a walk," he says to himself. A table lamp covered by a dirty brown shade throws a dim orange light through the cabin.

Walk. It's useless now.

Hugh turns off the light and switches on a flashlight. He directs the beam at Stephen and then himself. White dots explode under his closed lids. Stephen lifts his head.

Hugh, naked, bends near Stephen's feet. He unties the rope that binds his prisoner's legs, but leaves the mouth covered and his arms bound. "Get off the bed. Walk slowly."

Stephen lifts his legs, touches his feet to the floor. His knees wobble.

Hugh pushes the knife into Stephen's back and guides him through the cabin past the old beige couch, past the pictures— one of Jesus, one of Hitler—to the door.

The flashlight sweeps through the trees into the surrounding night. Hugh tilts his head backwards, but all he sees is blackness. The stars are obliterated by trees. The air is warm and damp and smells of pine. His feet scrape against rocks and dead branches.

A cemetery marker stands ghostly and gray in a clearing. The flashlight beam bounces off the dusky stone, illuminating the small cross at its peak. Hugh leads Stephen around a low rock wall to a slope that descends into the darkness. The beam hits the wooden crosses that rise into the night from the earthen mound.

Stephen gags into the tape.

Hugh sighs and says, "Don't drown."

He grabs Stephen's shoulders, forcing him to a stop, and pushes him down to his knees.

The flashlight sweeps up the mound where the two men hang on the crosses. Already their skins are bloated; black streaks trail from their mouths down their chests. Hugh plays the light across the empty cross.

He kneels and pulls Stephen close. "Father, forgive me, for I did not kill my brother. You did." He clutches the knife, pulls back Stephen's head and guides the weapon down his prisoner's chest.

My brother.

Stephen pisses involuntarily.

The knife swoops to Stephen's throat and the flow of urine stops.

"Filthy. Don't pollute the land. You've polluted your body with your filth. Dirty."

Stephen goes rigid.

Jesus in the Garden. Let us pray.

"Here is my body," Hugh intones with reverence. He raises his left hand to Stephen's face and swabs his fingers over the swollen eyes. He touches the face gently at first, feeling rough stubble on the cheeks—it reminds him of his father—then his fingers turn stiff and rough. His hand squeezes Stephen's jaw tighter until he thinks the bone may break. "Here is my body." Hugh forces his thumb through the tape into Stephen's mouth, pushes it forward, then the knuckles, until his hand disappears in the extended cheeks.

Footsteps rushed down the hall.

The door opened.

*"Get that goddamn thing out of your mouth," his father
screamed. "Little faggot! Who showed you how to do this?"*

*His little brother withdrew before his father slapped him hard
across the head. Then his father pushed his hand into his little
brother's mouth and tried to rip out his tongue.*

"I'll kill you both. Teach you little faggots."

*Hugh cowered with fear, guilt, and shame. "It's not my fault,"
he cried out. "Some older kids showed me. We were just playing
around."*

*"Playing," his father screamed, hitting them both blindly.
"Who's teaching you to be queers. Wash out your mouth. Wash
it out!"*

*His father smacked his little brother so hard his head smashed
against the footboard. Then there was silence and only the sound
of his father's panting and the smell of beer from his drooling
mouth.*

*"You little shit," his father said to him. "Goddamn it. It's all
your fault."*

*His little brother lay still, his flesh turning a light blue. Urine
seeped from his penis and blood trickled from his mouth.*

*"Nothing," his father warned. "You ain't seen nothing, or
you're dead."*

Stephen vomits onto Hugh's hand and falls forward, choking.

"I'm sorry," Hugh whispers. "You have to pay because no one
wants...."

He turns his captive over. Stephen's legs are black with dirt.
Weak. Easy. Faggot.

Hugh brings the rock down upon the dark head.

Stephen shivers and flops onto his side, his knees tucked up to
his waist like a child in bed.

Hugh drags Stephen to the cross. He has the man the world
wanted—the man he thought Carl wanted. Hugh will make the

world whole again. The Trinity will be complete. It will take time, but he will lift him so he takes his place among the others.

Golgatha will burn and its ashes will cover the ground like dark snow.

CHAPTER EIGHTEEN

I TRIED AN OLD MILITARY MANEUVER. I CUT INTO
the woods and then reversed direction toward the advancing
enemy lines. I weaved through the pines, being careful to stay in
the shadows, ever aware of the security systems I might be tripping.

A large two-story wooden farmhouse, lights ablaze, rose from
a clearing about a quarter of a mile from the cabin. A massive
stone tower loomed over one corner of the house. Carl was
correct about his fixation with gardening. Richly textured flower
beds and carefully pruned bushes in a lawn as manicured as a
country estate surrounded the house. I avoided the compound by
following the tree line. I came to a narrow dirt driveway which
ed away from the trucks and cars parked out front. My right
nkle burned like hell and the pain shot up my leg until it felt like
knife was stabbing me with every step.

In a few minutes, I was at the entrance I had spotted earlier in
e day. There was a smaller gate by its side which opened from
e inside. I decided to take a chance and go through the small
te, hoping to take advantage of the confusion surrounding my

escape. I shot through the gate and then hobbled toward the car. It took me another fifteen minutes of pained walking in the relative safety of the roadside ditch, over rocks and tree limbs, to get to the lumber road and the Cavalier.

As I reached for the door, a sudden fear clutched me. I reached into my right pocket; the keys to the Chevy were nestled in my jeans. Maybe Carl and Adam and the others didn't want to reach into a faggot's pants. Lucky me. I opened the trunk and pulled out my bag with my .357 inside. I unlocked the car, slid into the seat and looked in the rear-view mirror. My face was Halloween perfect. The right side was purple and swollen; dried blood coated the cuts from splinters. My left eye sported a fisticuffs shiner. Not the kind of face I wanted to show in public. My T-shirt was spotted with blood; my jeans ripped.

Mercifully, the Cavalier's ignition fired when I turned the key. The dashboard clock read 8:45 p.m. I headed south toward Boston.

I dreaded the phone call, but Win Hart answered.

"Whoa, where the hell are you?"

"Ronald McDonald land." I was looking through the shiny windows of a McDonald's south of Manchester from an outside payphone booth. A bored teenage girl scrubbed the chrome fixtures behind the counter and her male companion emptied the trash bins and wiped down plastic trays.

"Well, honey, you better get your Big Mac back in town if you want to save your ass. Everybody, including John, thinks you're lower than rat shit."

"How is John?"

"Depressed. Sad. Lonely. You name it. I've been staying over some nights. Seems to help."

"You're a good friend, Win."

Win sighed. "John needs a friend—one who'll find Stephen.

I suppose that's what you've been up to." He paused. "Stephen's parents flew in from Kansas today. It was nothing but weeping and wailing this evening. John was so fucked up he took a tranquilizer and went to bed. The parents went out to find something to eat, probably black-eyed peas and grits. These folks are the salt of the earth."

"Spinetti been around?"

"Why did you pull that shit with Spinetti? He told John he was going to find you and put you away for good."

"Figures."

"I don't know if I should tell you this, but the cops are keeping an eye on your apartment in case you show up. They got the keys from the landlord and threw everything you owned into plastic bags. Then they hauled it off. Detectives did it here, too. Chris had his hands in all of it."

The lights flickered off in the McDonald's. "Win, I can't explain this now, but tell John something for me. It's important. Tell him I'm looking for Stephen, and tell him not to talk to Chris or see that scumbag again. Tell him to make up any excuse, but don't let Spinetti in the door again."

"Des, John isn't going to go for any more mystery. This isn't a movie."

"Tell him I've got a hunch."

"Your hunches are lethal."

"Trust me. I'm trying to find Stephen. And I'm not the Combat Zone Killer."

Win sighed. "Sorry. I acted like a dick. When I had time to think, I figured you were telling the truth—but John's still not going to be happy."

I replied, "Very few of us are these days," and hung up the phone. I watched as the two McDonald's employees locked the doors, got into their cars, and drove away, leaving me standing alone under the glare of a floodlight.

* * *

Chris Spinetti's voice haunted me. Had I heard him at the compound or was I hallucinating? Hallucination or not, my next move was to search for clues in Chris's back yard.

Chris lived alone on the top floor of a triple decker in East Boston, a gray house on a dull street, made even duller by the night. I had memorized the address from the utility bill in Chris's office.

At a corner convenience store, bathed in fluorescent light, a few Italian boys dressed in street jeans and open shirts gathered outside with their girlfriends; otherwise, the neighborhood was as deserted as a cemetery on Saturday night.

I knew breaking into Chris's apartment would be a risk as big as, if not bigger than, burglarizing a building on Commonwealth Ave. East Boston, separated from Boston by the Mystic River, was tight. A community built by generations of immigrant families, most of them from Italy. A stranger would be noticed, unlike the busy, anonymous streets of the city. East Boston was changing, Cambodians, other immigrants, were moving in, but the old lady next door would still recognize every neighbor's footstep, know every sound on the summer breeze. Perhaps I'd get lucky and a late-night takeoff from Logan would cover my noise.

I drove by the address on Carver Street before I parked a block away. The apartment looked dark and uninhabited, but I walked past it to make sure the lights were still off. A staircase, a zig-zag contraption attached to the side of the building, led directly to the third-floor door.

Tonight, the windows of East Boston were open and life was relaxed and sleepy. I heard Jay Leno and laughter. I imagined portly men and women in their Barcaloungers smoking cigarettes and snacking on prosciutto in front of the television. A breeze had kicked in from the harbor and filled the air with the tangy smell of salt. It was a night for a walk on the beach with a lover, an activity much more wholesome than my current endeavor.

The triple decker was quiet and, for the most part, dark. I lifted the catch on the chain-link fence, which often marked the property line between the cramped houses, and scooted down a narrow cement walk scattered with plastic buckets and oversized tricycles. A dog next door, the fluffy yappy kind, barked and shoved its muzzle against a window screen. I hurried up the stairs, which creaked softly as I climbed to the third floor. The screwdriver I'd carried from the car, in case I needed to jimmy the door, was unnecessary. It was unlocked. Oh, to live in a crime-free neighborhood.

I found myself in Chris's kitchen. Detective Spinetti wasn't the best housekeeper. A weak light poured in the windows from a streetlamp. Three metal pots, one filled with the stringy remains of pasta, sat on the white stove. Long-handled spoons stuck out of the pots like crooked masts.

Piles of paper were scattered across a wooden kitchen table. Squinting, I sifted through them. Case files. Witness depositions. Nothing about Stephen. I moved on through the dark rooms.

The apartment was furnished a la 1970s college dorm. Apparently, the divorce had hit Chris hard in the wallett. I glanced inside the bedroom. A mattress rested on the floor. Clothes and underwear were tossed about the room. The red digital numbers of an alarm clock glared at me. It was just before midnight.

Three stacks of books formed small pillars in the dining room. Most were police procedural novels and true crime stories. In the corner, a metal shelving unit, the kind you could buy at any discount store, held personal mementos: three plastic bowling trophies, a framed picture of two girls (probably his daughters), other family photographs, a rosary, a leather weight belt, two plastic dumbbells, and, on the top shelf, a collection of knives lay barely visible. Switchblades, Bowie, bayonets, Ninja throwing, long-blade, short-blade. Chris had them all.

A white cloth pushed to the back caught my eye.

I lifted one end of the cloth and the object clattered onto the metal. It was the SS dagger Stephen had shown me the previous Saturday. I held it and it sparkled in the dim light like a faint star. I read the inscription on the blade, *Meine Ehre Heisst Treue*, and remembered the translation—My Honor is Loyalty. There was no plastic Baggie or evidence tag. My pulse quickened and the old paranoia closed in around me. I wrapped the knife back in its cloth and stuck it in my back pocket next to the screwdriver. They poked into my lower back like splints.

"Time is short, Des," Stephen had told me when we first talked in his apartment. "I'm talking to Chris because he takes these things seriously." Too seriously.

The yard sale theme carried over to the living room. It held an overstuffed sofa, an ancient television, a furry throw rug, and a dilapidated leather wing chair with stuffing bursting out of the arms. There was a small room to the side that looked as if it had been a closet at one time. A wooden chair and desk, again piled with papers, took up the space. This was Chris's idea of an office.

I heard a knock and stood silent, my heart pounding in my ears. Then, the kitchen door creaked open.

"Chris?" an older woman asked in a suspicious tone. The landlady? Maybe she had heard the knife fall on the shelf. I held my breath as steps advanced into the kitchen but then retreated. The door closed with a soft click.

I backed away from the desk and my butt hit a knob. I turned and opened a cabinet door I hadn't spotted before. Piles of magazines and video tapes were piled in front of me. It was too dark to tell what they were, so I had to take a chance and turn on the light. A bare bulb hung above my head, along with a dangling cord. I pulled it and a painful glare filled the office.

My God.

Hundreds of gay pornographic magazines and video tapes filled the space. Men coiled, writhing, snaked into every sexual position. Sinuous arms and legs, erections, asses. Solos. Duets. Threesomes. Groups. Leather. B&D. S&M. Fetish. Fisting. Something for every taste. I was getting close. The secrets had to come out.

A black attaché case sat next to a pile of the magazines. I used the screwdriver to wrench the locks and the case flipped open.

I knew the man in the Polaroid photographs inside—the young body with a face older than his age. The small scar under the lip, the nose slightly crooked from a break, showed clearly in the photos. He was the naked man lounging on the overstuffed couch in Chris's living room. His ass was in the air on the mattress in Chris's bedroom, and, in another taken from above, he held a long, thin penis over his face.

Clay Krieger. I knew the face, the body, the tattoo on his wrist—*Aryan America*.

I was saddened because the lure and danger of the street had killed Clay. It could have been me except for the gunshot that changed my life. And I was angry because a man—worse yet, a man of authority—had used him. Sad and angry, but nothing surprised me anymore. I doubted if Chris had paid Clay—he might have—more likely he threatened him, pulled out the badge and said, "Put out or your ass will be in jail instead of around my cock." And Clay didn't get fucked.

I grabbed a few of the more revealing photographs and put them in my pocket.

I was about to close the briefcase when I noticed a ragged edge of white paper in one of the folder pockets. I examined the handwriting, the tears along its side and I knew it fit perfectly into Stephen's diary.

I had all I needed from Chris Spinetti.

I wound through the house, out the kitchen and down the

stairs to the street. I didn't care whether I ran into Chris
I was armed.

Why not stay as close as possible to Chris? The great detective
might not think to look down the block, theorizing that I was
out of the Commonwealth, maybe out of the country by now.
Tomorrow, he would be right.

The Mayflower Motel in East Boston was tucked away near
the Wonderland dog track. I needed a nearby overnight stay
because I was too tired to drive. I planned to soak in a hot
tub, put ice on my face, sleep, and leave at check out time the
next morning. The bored check-in attendant looked as rough as
I did.

Stephen and I were making headlines now according to the
papers stuffed in the boxes outside the motel lobby. *Search for
Missing Journalist Continues*. And in even smaller type inside,
Bodyguard Sought/For Questioning/In Combat Zone Murders.
Fortunately, there was no photograph (they would have been hard
pressed to find one) or police sketch. Boston was getting far too
dangerous.

Tomorrow, I planned on ditching the car in a Logan parking
lot and then catching the next bus or train I could get to New
York City.

My room at the Mayflower had the unappetizing odor of a
warm, moldy sewer. I laughed at the curly pubic hairs on the
sheets because I was too tired and hungry to cry. Despite all my
efforts, I was back on the lam. Everything in my life seemed to
turn to shit no matter what I did.

I opened the bathroom window to let in some of the cooler
ocean air. My room faced the harbor rather than 1A. The tub was
stained a disgusting orange from a dripping faucet, but I filled it
and crawled in anyway. The warm water lapped over my legs and
chest, and soothed my aches and bruises. I had wrapped ice from

a chugging old machine near the check-in office in newspaper and held it, in turns, to my right ankle and face. I dozed off and when I jerked awake, I remembered the page I had taken from Chris's attaché case.

I was in love with Rodney Jessup.

I read the sentence again, my stomach sinking.

I was in love with Rodney Jessup. John is a fine partner—I couldn't ask for better. John is kind, compassionate, and good, but how many of us know the pain of one love that cannot, or will not, be ours. I was plagued by an obsessive, overpowering love that would not go away. I had lost the man I loved and he was all I could think about. In the first year, the memories would send my heart reeling. I thought I had lost that feeling forever until the day John and I spotted him on television.

I didn't want to believe it. These old feelings weren't supposed to come back. At the same time, I hated Rodney for what he had become. I had to tell John something, so I told him about the death threats, the investigation into Aryan America. These seemed like reasonable triggers for my sulky behavior.

After two months of trying to get through, I finally got the call I'd been waiting for. He pretended not to remember me. "Then why did you call me back, Rodney?" I asked. You never told me your real name. Go back, Rodney, to the Hercules Theater in New York City, 1978.

"I don't know what you're talking about," he said.

"I think you do."

We met again on June 10th. John thought I was in D.C. for a job interview. Rodney agreed to meet me for a few hours to discuss this "absurd case of mistaken identity," as he called it. I believed he wanted to see me as badly as I wanted to see him. I took a cab during a thunderstorm to an address he gave me in Arlington. I was standing under a black umbrella in an alley behind a deserted gas station. He pulled up in a black Mercedes.

He smiled and looked just the same—a little older—and the blood rushed to my head.

I turned the page over.

In two hours, he never acknowledged our beginnings. He didn't have to, it was clear he enjoyed being near me. We drove to a park somewhere and he rolled down the windows and opened the sunroof. We watched the dark clouds rumble overhead. He pulled at his tie and opened his shirt. I wanted to touch the skin around his neck, but I couldn't.

I asked him if he believed all those things he said on television. He said, "Yes, but I'm not a monster." He talked about his postcard life, but he also spoke of the "heavy hand of God" upon his family—Carol's two miscarriages – punishment for his sins.

"I kept your card," I said. "It fell out of your pocket at the Hercules." He jerked his head toward me, his eyes round and frightened. He started the car and drove me back to the gas station without a word. I pleaded with him to acknowledge what had happened. I told him that if he could accept himself, he wouldn't hate me so much and I wouldn't have to do what I had to do. He told me it was a mistake to see me. He threw $500 at me and said to get a cab back to the airport—he'd pay for his mistake. I took the money and felt like a whore.

Finally, lightly, in pencil. *John's back.*

The page ended.

I dropped the ice into the water and pulled myself out of the tub.

NINETEEN

THE CABIN IS BLEAK AND QUIET.

The men no longer moan. The wind has dropped in the trees.

He turns on the radio, looks for a bite to eat, and wonders if the men on the crosses are hungry.

Stupid. How could they be hungry? They are dead. Carl won't come. No one will come and I will be alone. Father, why hast thou forsaken me?

He finds a can of tuna and wolfs it down. When he turns away from the sink, three men gather around his feet. They grab his toes and pull at his ankles. Hugh brushes the phantoms away, kicking and screaming.

"You can't hide," Stephen says. "They will find us and then they'll find you. You'll hang."

"No," he says and pushes Stephen away. He grabs an empty beer bottle from the table and throws it at Stephen's head. The three men vanish as quickly as they had appeared.

The quiet is shattering; the silence deathly.

Father, come for me. Please help me!

Hugh pulls the rifle from its case. The dream is over. The money lost.

He sticks the cold barrel in his mouth.

Why, father, why did you kill my brother, the only boy I ever loved? Why did you abandon me? Father? Comfortable, must get comfortable. But he alone—shut the door and windows.

Hugh doesn't notice the heat, how he shuts off the breeze. He strips off his jeans and puts on a flannel shirt, the one that reminds him of his brother. The one *he* killed through his unnatural urges.

"I didn't kill him," he cries out, but no one hears.

Comfortable.

A billfold rests on the table. Inside are forty-six dollars, a credit card, a Museum of Fine Arts membership, free passes to The Body Club, a driver's license, an insurance card. All the markers of life. Hugh realizes he has none of these. He never did.

He pulls out a card tucked into a slot in the front of the billfold. The name seems familiar.

No one will come.

He holds the card and sits in a chair next to the bed. He ties a string to the trigger and hooks it to his big toe. The rifle rests in the V of his groin, the barrel positioned for his mouth. He stretches out, legs bent slightly until the line pulls taut against the trigger. If he extends his legs further it will be over.

Comfortable.

Stephen and the other two men crawl toward him. Their mouths are bloated and blood drains from their lips. They pull on his toes, grab the hair on his legs.

The card—put the card away. He forgets the billfold is next to him on the floor. *The card means nothing. I'll put it back.* He laughs at the funny, useless detail that fills his mind.

Stephen's hands are reaching upwards now, pulling their way to his groin. He lifts his arm to reach for the billfold and Stephen bites his leg.

"Get off, motherfucker! Get off!"
He kicks at the demon on his leg.
The rifle explodes in his face.

TWENTY

ABOUT 10 A.M. THE NEXT MORNING, I PLACED A CALL
to Chris Spinetti.

I called from a pay phone at Logan International where I'd
ditched the Cavalier in the general parking garage. The day was
hot and windy and the airport was filled with summer travelers.
I wanted to escape in drag, but my face was still too bruised
and swollen and I suspected a man with a shiner would attract
less attention than a woman with the same injury. I covered the
bruises as best I could with makeup and hoped my efforts would
be sufficient. The rest of my disguise consisted of my baseball
cap to hide my hair and some cheap sunglasses purchased at an
airport gift shop.

The payphone was in the High Flight Lounge. I watched an
Aer Lingus 747 taxi down the shimmering runway. The lounge
looked anything but high this morning. A few subdued patrons
picked at their breakfast. The liquor bottles lined up behind the
bar called seductively to me. I had a sudden thirst for gin, the
devil of all spirits. Instead, I took a bite of a mushy bagel.

"District Four," a polite female voice answered.

"Detective Spinetti, please."

The phone clicked and after what seemed like hours, the voice I knew blurted into my right ear, tense and annoyed. "Spinetti."

"Spaghetti?" I let the word drool from my mouth.

There was a long pause and then the phone slammed hard onto something on the other end. I assume it was Chris's desk. The line buzzed and I thought I'd lost the connection.

"You little fuck." The words sounded as if they had been plucked from hell, pronounced by the Furies.

"That's no way to address a gay brother, Chris."

"I'll kill you."

"Nice dick. The doctor did a good job on the circumcision."

Chris bayed like a hound.

"Calm down," I said, after his anger lessened from nuclear to boil. "You can always make porn if you lose your job on the force."

He swore at the phone. "I need a trace," he yelled to someone at District.

"Don't bother. I'll tell you exactly where I am. Logan." I stuck a cigarette in my mouth, but didn't light it. He stopped screaming. "I'm not going to be here long, and anyway, I don't think you really want to send any of those straight cop friends of yours to come get me, if you think about what I'm carrying."

"What do you want?" The question was cautious, but filled with anger.

"Answers. In person."

"You broke into my apartment."

"The door was open."

"Where? When and where?" He sounded cornered, like a man forced at gunpoint to walk off a cliff, and I shook a little at the danger I'd created; yet, I knew I had to meet it head on.

"The sooner the better. Someplace we both know and love."

"Where's that?" he snapped.

"Thank about it. Give me an hour to get there."

I hung up the phone and caught the subway into Boston.

For the second time that morning, I considered falling off the wagon. I ordered a corned beef sandwich at a deli on the edge of the Zone and thirsted for a tall glass of pilsner beer. The beer would give me the added strength I needed to face Chris. One might lead to another, until I'd be so shitfaced, I'd walk away from this madness and everybody would be better off. Or, I'd be so drunk, I'd shoot the bastard on sight. However, under the consideration that Chris—surely homicidal by now – might shove his Glock in my face when I walked in the door, I reconsidered the drink. The days of wine and roses would have to wait. My lips remained chaste.

Just before noon, I walked into the netherworld of the Déjà Vu with my black bag in hand. The attendant was a dark-skinned woman in a blue suit and red gaucho hat. Her perfume masked the musky smells of the theater. She smiled, wished me a good day, and went back to reading her *People* magazine. She didn't give my duffel a second glance; apparently, management accepted patrons who carried in toys, liquid lunches or whatever other accessories they might need to enjoy the show, including guns.

My eyes needed to adjust, so I waited in a dim corner of the lobby. Once inside, I watched fifteen minutes of an orgy in *Chateau de Passion*, before attempting a look around. I had to admit the French men were hairy and handsome and the women were in the range of a gay man's acceptability, thin with small breasts, but for me the film might as well have been *Bambi*. Sex really wasn't on my mind.

I took a seat in a dark last row, which was protected from behind by a high wooden divider separating the theater from the lobby. The seat I chose gave me an unobstructed view of anyone entering or leaving from either the left or right aisles. I opened my bag, took out the .357, loaded it, and rested it on my lap.

Even in this relatively early hour of porn-sex, I counted at least 50 men in the house. A smoker hacked several rows in front of me. My seat was central enough no one approached me and that was the way I wanted it. The French video ended and *Dressed to Thrill*, a poorly made S&M fetish reel, flickered on the screen.

I sat for five hours, half-watching the porn double bill and scrutinizing the men who glided like ghosts down the aisles. The onscreen sex bored me, and, after a time, white dots danced before my eyes. I had to go downstairs to piss. I grabbed my bag and headed to the toilets from hell.

Activity was light in the bathroom. Three men crowded into one of the stalls in a cramped union of cock sucking. One, a fortyish man with a bald head and gray mustache, waved me in. I politely declined, but admired his democratic principles, and stood next door at the toilet while they happily carried on, pushing and straining against the green metal.

After several more hours, I was getting a complex, not to mention hunger pangs. No one had even looked at me. I knew the situation was getting desperate when I started analyzing the reasons for my unattractiveness: age, beauty, disgusting bruises, etc. Maybe it was the vibes I was throwing off.

Finally, a pleasant grocery store manager from Newton, who said he only wanted to talk, crawled into the seat next to me. At first, I welcomed the company, but after an hour of inane conversation, I politely told him I wasn't interested and he skulked off.

A few minutes later, the man I was looking for sauntered down the right aisle. He was dressed in a dark shirt and jeans and walked casually, with the ease of a veteran cruiser—more like the ease of a veteran cop—but I could have been overestimating his nonchalance in the gloom. I wondered if my impulsiveness to get into Boston might have been a strategic failure. Chris held the advantage. I was tired, hungry, and edgy after an eight-hour stay in the Déjà Vu. Chris, on the other hand, looked focused and confident. I turned away from him and ducked as low as I could go as he passed. I didn't want to give away my advantage.

The detective slid into a seat next to a man about ten rows in front of me. They turned their heads toward each other and then turned away. They stared at the screen for about five minutes. Chris lit a cigarette and the smoke curled up into the hazy flicker of light. The detective slid his left arm around the other man's shoulders and then nuzzled against the man's neck. He shifted slightly and moved his right arm toward the other man. The cop's head disappeared into the man's lap. The recipient of his service relaxed and stretched back in his seat.

Spinetti had balls. He was acting like nothing mattered but his own sex drive. Anger surged through me.

I could kill him and splatter his brains over the other man. The .357 would make quite a mess. The blowjob was over, I decided. *Coitus interruptus.* I hitched the duffle over my left shoulder and sprinted toward the two men. The detective's head bobbed in short strokes.

I stopped Chris with the muzzle of the .357.

He gagged.

"Holy shit," the other man said. It was the Newton grocer.

"It's okay," I said. "We're lovers and we play this little game all the time. He tricks out and I catch him, and, in a jealous rage, I rape him in front of the assembled crowd. He loves it. We've done it for years. Want to join in?"

"Jesus, no," the grocer replied.

"Well, honey," I said to Chris, "time to go home. Nobody wants to play. Might as well stop getting your throat swabbed."

Chris raised his head slowly off the rather thick piece of meat. This grocer's basket was ample.

"Game's not over, Des." Chris's voice was resigned, flat.

"Could you excuse us, please," I said to the grocer. "I think we're about to have a lovers' quarrel."

"Gladly," the grocer said. He zipped up his fly and darted off in the darkness.

I shielded the gun with my left hand, pushed it into the nape of Chris's neck and maneuvered my way to the seat behind him. "I say the game's done, Chris."

"I've been a fool, Des. This goes deeper than you know. More than you or I can handle. I knew you'd be here. I thought I might as well enjoy myself one last time before looking for you. I mean, what's the rush? You hold all the cards now."

"Where's Stephen?"

Chris laughed.

"No laughing matter," I said. I pushed the gun deeper into his neck and he pushed back hard, as if he relished the feel of it on his skin. "I look at it this way. You broke into Stephen's apartment after you found out he was missing. You wrote the message on the screen. He told you too much. He came to you for help and you used everything he told you against him. You called Rodney Jessup to let him know about Stephen's speech. Let me use my psychic gifts here, Chris. Let me divine the answer. You would deliver Stephen Cross to the devil for half-a-million dollars."

He shook his head and I told him not to move.

"You have no fucking clue, Des. Half-a-million is small time. Half-a-mil is what some anonymous nutcase made up to put the fear of God into Stephen Cross. Try four times that."

"Jessup's the only one who could come up with that kind of money. Jessup paid you two million dollars for Stephen? That's a nice take. Sure beats a detective's salary."

He laughed again and my trigger finger got itchy.

"Hurry up, Chris. Every second, I get closer to killing you." I wanted to kill him, if not for me, for Stephen. I hoped he wouldn't test me because the choice would be easy. However, the thought struck me that maybe the worst punishment for Spinetti would be to crash his gay closet—throw open the doors and fling him out. Sad to say, I could end his life with a couple of phone calls as easily as I could with a bullet. A few conversations with his District Chief, his ex-wife, mother and father in the North End would be enough, or I could pull the trigger. But what of all those years distinguishing myself? I was proud of the things that had been taken away from me: my book collection, my records, my leather. But I was even more proud of what couldn't be taken away: good drag, my intelligence, my willingness to learn, my sexuality, my *gayness*. My previous lives of dealing and hustling had tarnished *the me* that Chris was so quick to see and judge. Why add murder to my small list of negatives?

"No, I didn't deliver Stephen to Rodney Jessup," Chris said. "All I wanted was the money. I believed Stephen from the beginning because he's the kind of guy who doesn't bullshit. He's smart and honest. And if he was telling the truth, there was a lot of money to be made."

"Stephen told a few lies. You read his diary."

"Blackmail, brother. That's all I wanted. A little payoff to destroy evidence. Rodney's happy—he buys his candidacy. Stephen doesn't get hurt—he comes off like some faggot crackpot. I just had to get my hands on the proof. That was all. I got close with the diary, but I couldn't find the goddamn business card, the one with Jessup's name on it."

"Then who got to Stephen?" The face of a young tough, the soldier in my dream, rushed into my head.

"Who knows? Someone working for Jessup? The psycho who's carving up hustlers? Stephen had enemies. That made the whole thing easier—why it was so easy to pin it on Aryan America. So many people had a reason to hate Stephen, the way they have so many to hate a fag."

The screen went dark. Chris reached into his pockets.

"Keep it straight," I said.

"A cigarette."

I leaned to his left with the gun still pressed to his neck. The lighter flashed and the dark mustache and handsome profile came into view. A woman in a latex body suit holding a horse whip appeared on the screen and *Dressed to Thrill* came on for the fifth time since I had walked in.

"I wish I could have kept it straight," Chris said with a deep exhale. He lowered his head and the .357 pulled away from his neck. "Jessup didn't know who the hell I was, but the moment I called and said I wanted to talk about Stephen Cross, he knew. He knew things were going to get rough. Maybe he made one mistake—one that haunted him—and he believed, like a drunk who says one more before he gets behind the wheel, that the past doesn't really matter. It was so long ago and he prayed the mistake would go away. Nobody would know. He really believed the Hercules wouldn't come back to haunt him."

Chris shook his head. "The trouble with you and Stephen is that you're too much in-your-face homos for the rest of us. Jessup's probably thinking, why for Christ's sake didn't that fag die of AIDS? Why not Stephen Cross? Think of the anxiety Jessup had to live with. His first time on television, always expecting the day a reporter would run over and say, 'There's a rumor about you, Reverend Jessup,' and it would be over. He could deny it—there was no hard evidence—or he could confess, but that would kill him, too, because then he'd be one of those *weak* men who made a big mistake. Either way he'd be screwed. He'd jump awake at 4 a.m. with a scream and that lovely blonde thing of a wife would bring him cold compresses and change the sheets when his sweat would soak the bed. He could never be himself. Can you imagine trying to hide all those years?"

"Like you?"

He pushed his head back against the gun.

"You took the easy way out, Des. Guys like you have it made. You come out and you don't give a fuck. I got a family, kids, a career. You don't know the hell I've been through, pushing back this sickness I thought I had. It's harder for us—the ones in the closet. The ones like me, the ones who have to keep it all inside. We make it safe for you because society can't put its finger on us. Is he gay? Is he straight? The guys you take a shower with can't call you a fag because they can't tell. If they're wrong it comes back so close it bites them in the ass. We keep those guys off you.

"But I can't sit in a gay bar and talk about dance clubs and hair styles and Judy Garland. I don't have that luxury. The Déjà Vu was the only place that was kind to me. In the dark, I could be the biggest queer on earth and nobody gave a fuck. I didn't have to take faggot this and faggot that and all that ball-busting testosterone shit. I met Clay here. He was nice. I was sorry he died. I had to act like I wasn't because of all my straight brothers would think I was queer. Hauling you in for the Combat Zone murders would get the news off Stephen, make my life a little easier. But now you know, Des. I'm a cocksucker and I'm dead.

"I got bills to pay, loans and debts to people you can't even imagine. And the worst part is, I got two beautiful girls who can't even stand to look at me because their mother tells them what a creep I am. And now, add insult to injury. I wanted them to grow up proud of me, proud because I was a cop. Proud because I was a man. You think dealing with Catholic parents is fun? And you think I can come out? I'd never see any of them again." He sighed. "Two million dollars. A future for my girls. It would take me a long way from here, maybe somewhere where I could—"

"—You are a man. Hide and seek is a kid's game, Chris. We can get up and go to the police, tell them what we know and maybe it won't be too late for Stephen or for us. Your kids will still love you. Think of them. You can work this out."

He lowered his head into his hands and sobbed. A woman moaned on screen.

"Jessup," he muttered between sobs. "The thugs in New Hampshire. One of them will be out for me, and then you and the rest of us. They'll kill me and then they'll kill you."

My heart softened a bit for him. "They can't kill all of us."

"Sure they can. It's easy to find us now. Gay gyms, bars, magazine subscriptions, mail-order lists. They can round us up."

"Closet's getting to you, Chris. Let's go."

He shivered in the seat.

I let my guard down in a moment of sympathy. I thought he reached down for another cigarette—I was wrong. Before I knew it, he had knocked my hand away and he was standing in the row in front of me, the Glock pointed at my face.

"The game's not over, Des," he said. The sobs had turned to growls.

A man and woman exploded in an orgasm on screen.

I shrunk back in my seat, put the Magnum in my lap and said, "Think about this, Chris. Murder doesn't become you."

"It would be so easy to kill you."

His voice chilled me.

"How lucky that I ran into the Combat Zone killer in the Déjà Vu. No one would question why I had to put a bullet in your head."

"Well, probably no one, except for one small detail," I said. "I gave your pictures, Stephen's diary, and a note about what to make of this mess to a friend. I told him that if he didn't hear from me within twenty-four hours to mail the whole package to John Dresser. I even provided the stamps." I lied, but it was my only hope of getting out of the Déjà Vu alive. The pictures and Stephen's diary were in the duffle next to me.

The breath drained out of Spinetti. "Well, it was worth a shot. You always were one step ahead. You see, Des, either way I can't live like this—a fucking despised gay man—or a murderer. That's why I needed to enjoy the Déjà Vu one last time."

The Glock went up to his right temple.

A flash burned through the darkness; the retort deafened my ears. I heard garbled voices that said nothing and everything. My eyes swam in the light, then the light disappeared and I shook in the dark. Chris had fallen forward, his bloody head coming to rest on the back of the seat, not three feet from my lap.

Footsteps and men shouting. Warm, sticky liquid covered my face. The bullet had blown a hole through his head and blood was leaking from his nose and mouth. I stumbled out of my seat, my stomach convulsing. I drew in some slow breaths to calm my panic, to think. Chris's blood had splattered into my mouth, filtered up my nose.

I heard sirens in the distance.

The handsome face was a black mass. The Glock had fallen underneath his feet. I rushed past him to an emergency side exit. The alarm wailed as I pushed open the door and stepped into the dark.

My black bag was my only friend.

I sprinted down the fire lane on my gimpy leg and made my way through the maze of alleys in Chinatown. I needed to get the blood off my body and clothes, and the only thing I could think to do was to throw myself into Fort Point Channel, a murky extension of Boston Harbor about ten minutes away.

The streets were mostly empty. If a car passed by, I held the bag in front of my body and lowered my head. I found a dock off a deserted pier. Behind me, the city skyline twinkled in the night.

I plunged into the dark water, as cold as slick metal, way too cold. The air fled from my lungs and my arms flailed against the surface. Chunks of ice floated around me *in the vat* and an arm from the deep grabbed my leg as I thrashed about. The arm pulled me under and I saw Chris, his face a bloody pulp, his skin shimmering with a purple wetness. He grabbed my throat. My lungs were bursting; my brain on the verge of a blackout.

I fought and kicked until I got his hands off my throat and my head above water. Then, I coughed out the foul liquid, grabbed the pier and held on. Beneath me, the hands slipped from my legs. I climbed up a rickety metal ladder and sat on the dock and rubbed my face hard to get the blood off. My cheeks were numb when I finally stopped and stared into the lights rippling across the water.

In a sparkling wave ten feet from the dock, a hand broke the surface like a hungry fish and then sank into the dark depths.

CHAPTER TWENTY-ONE

I SETTLED INTO A DARK BASEMENT APARTMENT
near 10th Avenue and 47th Street, Hell's Kitchen. My new landlord, whom I caught buying crack cocaine under the marquee at
the Martin Beck Theater one early Sunday morning in late July,
was the only one I figured who wouldn't look at me like I was
trash, dismiss me or ask for a driver's license or passport.

He only wanted cash.

Even though it was cheap, the first month's rent wiped out
about half my money. The apartment was a dump: greasy
appliances, unpainted walls, spindly-legged skeletons of cock-
roaches in the bathtub. It wasn't nearly as nice as my digs in
Boston, but somehow it fit my mood—a rat in hiding, holing up
for the approaching fall and winter. I missed the stuff I left up
north. Fortunately, I still had my Shakespeare, which I found
in New York years ago, wrapped in a paper bag near 110th and
Amsterdam, destined for the garbage truck.

Every afternoon at about two, the sun would flood through the
tiny 47th Street window for twenty minutes. The light depressed

me because I knew the sun would be so low in the sky in a couple of months, I'd get no sun until the corresponding angle returned—if I still lived there.

The night of Spinetti's death, I slept under a railroad bridge near South Station. The next morning, I caught a train into New York City, Penn Station. On the ride, I read a front-page story about the suicide of a police detective in the Combat Zone, but Spinetti's death was never linked to Stephen Cross. Police wanted to question "a man in a baseball cap"—me—seen talking to the detective before his death. I suspected the Newton grocer wasn't involved in that tip. I was confident the police didn't have a lot to go on regarding my case as the "Combat Zone Killer," because Chris was fabricating evidence against me. Stephen's connection to Aryan America was another way to keep the detective involved in his disappearance. Any excuse to rifle through John and Stephen's belongings. He needed Rodney Jessup's card for the real payoff, and that search would have taken up most of his energy. I was an annoying mosquito, whom he almost trapped.

After a couple of nights on the street near Central Park, I decided to look for an apartment. Picking trash was the only option I had to make money. That and hustling had kept me in room and board when I had lived years ago in New York. A million treasures lie buried in New York garbage if you're brave enough to go after them. I was searching the trash on 45th Street when I met my landlord.

Life was blissfully dull for several months. The bruises and sprains from my run-in with Carl Roy had long subsided. In fact, I'd settled into a routine to build up my physical and emotional strength. The high-alcohol diet had disappeared years ago, too—now I went vegetarian and high protein. I ran at least five miles a day, most of the time around the tree-lined paths of Central Park, or up the broad waterway of the Hudson to the George Washington Bridge, sometimes down to Battery Park and the World

Trade Center, or the Lower East Side, in sight of the heavy spires of the Williamsburg Bridge. I found a bench and weights on 54th Street and dragged them down the seven blocks to my apartment. I lifted. I crunched. I pushed up. I lost 10 pounds and defined muscles to a cut I hadn't seen in several years. And I rested. Life was at my own pace and it was good.

Stephen was never far from my mind. The headlines about his disappearance had faded from the front page over the summer, and then dropped away entirely. As the season ended, the chances of Stephen being found alive diminished. In late August, I wrote to John, but mailed the letter from Philadelphia after a 90-minute train ride. I was still leery of anyone knowing exactly where I lived. I explained everything I knew: my meeting with Rodney Jessup, my happy trip to Carl Roy's, what I found in Chris's apartment and the final evening at the Déjà Vu. I left out two important details—Stephen's love for Rodney Jessup and mine for Stephen.

It took all my energy to put pen to paper. Everything in me resisted—but the blood was too near my hands. I imagined that John realized my fondness for Stephen and hated me for it, and somehow he might feel I was responsible for all that happened. In the letter, I assured him that I had nothing to do with Stephen's disappearance or the killings, and that I had acted to save Stephen's life (at least find him) as best I could. How much I really cared for Stephen, even loved him in my odd way, was left unsaid. I simply asked that John believe what was in the letter and that he trust me. I told him I would do my best to keep up the search. I also vowed never to turn myself in to the police for questioning. All any cop needed to know was spelled out in my handwriting.

* * *

A chilly October wind blew hard down the streets the day I finally called John. Rows of round white clouds with gray bottoms capped Manhattan's immensity. I had planned to call John once or twice before but only got as far as the end of my block.

I pulled my jacket collar around my neck and leaned against a payphone booth at the corner of 45th and 9th. It was about 2 p.m. on a Sunday afternoon, an hour before my dishwashing shift was to start at a Chinese eatery about three blocks from my apartment. I had seen a sign in the window in September and applied. Mr. Han, the owner, didn't ask questions. He paid me pretty well and I even got a share of tips.

As I punched in the number, I figured John would be at work with clients at The Body Shop. I preferred not to talk. The phone rang five times and then the answering machine picked up.

I left a short message: "Remember, if Adam Roy calls you, get a number or take down any message he gives you. I'm sorry about everything—most of all Stephen. I'll keep in touch." I wanted to say more, to tell John how sad I had been, how I felt Stephen's loss as much as he did, but I didn't think John would want to hear those words.

I walked to Greenwich Village and had a pot of tea.

* * *

I called again in December from an 8th Avenue subway platform. The silver cars of an A Train rumbled past. Black watery spots surrounded the base of the phone support and the air reeked of urine; however, I was happy to be out of the cold wind.

This time, John answered the phone. His voice was as icy as the day.

"Any word?" I asked.

"None." He paused. "You got a message here. Sounded like a young man. He left a number, but no name. He didn't identify himself as Adam Roy. I gave the detective on the case the number, but it turned out to be a crank call...a general store in New Hampshire. The owners didn't know anything. Jensen's the name. You might like him."

"Who?"

"The detective. Jensen."

"Sure," I said, uncomfortable with the subject of police. "How have you been?"

"Better. I'm leaving Boston." His voice thawed a little and shifted into sadness.

"I'm sorry."

"Yeah, after Christmas. I want to be out of here by New Year's Eve. You caught me packing."

I heard a shuffle on the line.

"I was looking through the photo albums before I put them in boxes. Stephen and me on the dunes at Herring Cove in Provincetown. Having dinner at our favorite table at Napi's. The Memorial Day barbecue in Kansas with Stephen's parents. Weeding my parents' garden last spring in Vermont. Me cleaning the fireplace, scrubbing the dishes, pouring detergent into the washer—"

His voice broke. The phone dropped and sobs echoed through the line.

"John," I said softly. "John?"

He came back on, angry. "Why is it the little things? Every damn little thing. Wiping the sink. Cleaning the tub. Drying silverware. All the little things we worked so hard for...."

"He loved you, John."

"I hope you're right, Des, because that's all I've got now—memories and a lot of little things and the *hope* that he loved me. I can't stand to think about Rodney Jessup and Stephen, even if Jessup denies it all. I *know* it happened. I'm angry with Stephen for not telling me and for allowing *this* to happen to us. I want Jessup dead and I hate myself for it."

He cried into the phone and I stood by, taking in his anger and pain. After he composed himself, I asked, "Where are you moving?"

"Someplace warm. Maybe my sister's in Pensacola for a while. I don't know how I'll get along down there being a Yankee, but she seems to like it." He sniffed and then chuckled. "Send me a letter. I'll leave a forwarding address once I know for sure."

I sighed and leaned against the post.

"I know you loved him, too," John said. "We both miss him."

His words burned in my ears and my throat tightened. We said goodbye and I didn't know whether I would ever talk to him again.

On the way back to my apartment, the cold stabbed into my face.

"Land's. How can I help you?"

I pictured the low peaks around Warren, the heavy oak door, the gray tiger cat preening on the wooden counter.

The voice, pleasant, a bit throaty, triggered memories of a pretty face—high cheek bones, deep brown eyes, brown hair in a trim cut. I said her name.

She paused.

"Yes. Who's this?"

"Des."

Another pause.

"You gave me directions to Carl Roy's place."

"Oh, my God," she said, her voice crackling with energy. "David! It's Des. He's on the phone."

David picked up on the other line. "Well, we didn't know if we'd hear from you again. Seems things got a bit weird up here."

"Speaking of weird," Ann said, "Adam Roy's one crazy kid. What happened?"

"No one got hurt, except for me—just a few bruises and a killer sprain."

"We get all the gossip at the store," David said, "but we keep our noses clean. It would be bad for business if we didn't. People can talk all they want, but we don't spread rumors. All hell broke loose the night you were here. We had more cops in town than I'd ever seen, all looking for the Combat Zone Killer. Apparently,

Carl thought he had you."

Ann, her voice still brimming with energy, said, "I told David, 'that guy isn't a killer.' I saw too many of them on the front page of the Hartford paper. At least, that's what I wanted to believe after my knees stopped shaking."

"Rest assured, I've never killed anyone," I said. "I was in some trouble way back, but nothing like that. A detective in Boston tried to set me up. He's dead."

The line fell into silence.

"The one who committed suicide last summer," I said.

Ann and David breathed again.

"Well, about a month ago," David continued, "Adam Roy left a letter here for you. He looked upset as hell. We asked him what was wrong. He said he needed to leave something for the man who caused all the trouble in July."

"They still think you're the killer," Ann said.

David said, "Adam couldn't talk about it. He said he was going to call a number in Boston and give that person our number, and someday we'd probably get a call from the Combat Zone killer."

"I thought Adam was going to cry," Ann said. "Usually that kid acts like he's got a pole strapped to his back. Anyway, he gave us the letter and told us to give it to you if we saw you. He made us promise never to tell his father or anyone else what was going on because if we did he'd be in real trouble, and please do him this favor and he'd be grateful." Ann paused. "He was sweet as pie. We want the Roys to be grateful to us."

"You could have called the police," I said. "Weren't you suspicious, at least curious?"

"Would a killer ask that?" Ann asked David. "I told you he wasn't a killer." Then she returned her attention to me. "No, I wasn't suspicious at all. I knew it in my gut."

"I was looking for a friend who still hasn't been found," I said.

"Listen," David said. "We know Carl's reputation. We've

201

sunk everything we own into this business. The Realtor failed to mention Carl Roy as one of Warren's features when we signed the purchase and sale. Carl's a neighbor. It's in our best interest to get along with the Roys. Adam included."

"Besides," Ann said, "the kid put a stamp on the letter even though he didn't have a name or address on it. Guess he thought it would be a federal offense for anyone to open his mail."

"It is, you know," David said.

Ann laughed. "Not that letter, David. It's not even legit."

"It doesn't matter now," I said. "I'll be up tomorrow to pick it up—if I can get a car."

"Dress warmly," Ann said. "We're up to our butts in snow."

I pleaded, cajoled, and begged my landlord for the use of his used Ford Tempo. He relented after I paid him $200 to use the car for three days. He had me. Anywhere else, I would need a fake DL to rent a car. I didn't want to take that risk. I also pleaded, cajoled, and begged to get three days off from work. Mr. Han wasn't happy, but I assured him it was a family emergency and I wouldn't walk away from the job.

I left about 5 a.m. on a Friday. The morning was raw and windy and white smoke curled from the Manhattan rooftops. It would be 20 degrees colder in the mountains. As I left the city behind, the patchy clouds broke apart during a pink sunrise, and, thereafter, a brilliant sun warmed my trip all the way to Warren.

I arrived about 11 a.m., in time for lunch. David, looked as mountain-man butch as ever. Ann, relaxed and comfortable as the country store proprietress, shook my hand and offered me a free turkey sandwich, which I gladly accepted. With mustard, lettuce and tomato. She remembered. To be fair, so my reputation might rise a bit in their eyes, I told them about Stephen's disappearance in abbreviated form, and what had happened since.

To spare them the gory details, I left out a few of the important aspects of the story.

After an hour of talking, with several interruptions from customers, David brought out the letter. It was in a plain white envelope with nothing on the front except a first-class stamp. I used the store restroom and said goodbye. I wanted to open the letter in the car, privately. I had no idea what to expect.

It was a note in large sprawling script and read:

Whatever I owe is paid up. You talked about Hugh. Hugh had to leave a long time ago, but he told me about his secret cabin in the woods. I remember where it is, but I can't sneak away without getting into big trouble. I think something really bad may have happened there. I know what it's like to lose friends.

Adam had drawn a crude map that gave directions to the cabin "way back" in the woods. The cabin of Hugh Mather.

The cabin was only a few miles from the Aryan America compound as the crow flew, but it was hard to reach. From Adam's map, I suspected there might be some difficulty, so I set out immediately to get there and back before sunset.

According to the directions, the cabin was located on the other side of the mountain near the site of an old Colonial cemetery. I needed to find a block granite hitching post on the side of the highway. I could park the car there, Adam noted, and walk back into the woods, probably a mile or so on fairly level terrain, until the mountain started to rise up. I would have to cross a stream. The cabin would then be on a small plain a short distance from the water.

I drove past the hitching post twice before I spotted it. Finally, I parked the car near the post in a cleared area; I didn't want to get the Tempo stuck in the snow. I was better prepared this time than in July. I had brought a backpack filled with snacks and bottled water. The .357 was in the trunk. Carrying the gun was easy this time because of the leather shoulder holster I'd purchased at a pawn shop on 9th Avenue. Carrying it seemed prudent this trip.

It was slow going through the calf-deep snow. Often, I'd sink up to my thighs in drifts. The snow was crystalline and pure, and, in the shadows of the trees, as deeply blue as twilight. In the bright sun, it blinded me like a million glittering stars. There was little sound or movement in the woods. The forest soothed me with its cold isolation. It welcomed me with the gentle sway of the pines in the wind and the solitary chirps of tiny birds. Their forked tracks lay upon the snow-covered branches. Now and then one would flush from the trees and a shower of powder would sprinkle to the ground. Squirrel tracks circled the trees; there were larger ones as well, probably of deer, but I couldn't be sure. Of one fact I was certain— no human had traveled this way since the last snowfall.

After about an hour of slogging through the forest, the land began to swing upward. Dark mounds of rock jutted from the slope ahead. I came to a stream, flowing fast and black under patches of ice. It was shallow enough I could wade across without getting water in my boots. The land rose steeply beyond the water, but it leveled off not more than 100 yards away. I hadn't missed one of Adam's landmarks.

The cabin was a black cube on a bed of white; savageness, I suspected, covered by a peaceful blanket. A foot of snow lay on the roof and the cabin's dark logs were splotched with patches of icy white.

I wasn't concerned about an ambush because no one knew I was coming except the Lands. However, I carefully surveyed every aspect of the cabin before I approached. It looked dead— there were no footprints around it.

A bench sat outside, its seat filled solid with crusty snow. A curved TV satellite dish enveloped in white sat behind the cabin, its receiver pointed away from the mountain.

I knocked on the door. Its small rectangular window was glazed with ice.

There was no answer, so I turned the knob, pushed the door open, and stepped inside.

Like the air, the cabin was freezing. My breath turned to smoke in front of me. A smell—like rotted meat, but stagnate and confined by the cold—filled the cabin.

I looked in horror around the room. Pictures of men from pornographic magazines, genitals cut and mutilated, were spread across the plank floor. Jesus and Hitler looked out from the wall. A table covered with books stood in front of me. On the other side, near the back wall, a chair and couch sat empty.

"Hugh?" I called.

Dark spots dotted the grimy bed sheets. Then, I saw a bony arm, stiff, fist clenched, jammed between the chair and the couch. I moved closer. A rifle sprouted from the floor like a frosty flag pole.

I peered down and the corpse of a man I didn't know came into view. It reminded me of pictures I'd seen of bodies at Auschwitz, withered, skeletal, mummy-like. The mouth, what was left of it, grinned in death. He was naked except for an open flannel shirt. A string was attached from the big toe of his right foot to the rifle's trigger. I made out the remains of a swastika on one of the few remaining pieces of withered flesh on the underside of his right arm. I didn't know him, but I felt like I had seen his face: the soldier who had shot the men in my dream. I shook in the cold and stared at the ragged flesh. The smell of death drifted into my nose.

This was Hugh. The Combat Zone Killer.

The cabin was his frozen tomb.

A cabin in the snow, a man on the slab, the coldness of the vat. Cold. I wanted the cold to numb me; instead, I coughed out the rancid air and fled.

I walked into the forest because I knew there was more to discover. My intuition pulled me in one direction, under the pines, past the bare branches of birches, deeper into the forest darkness. As I came to a cemetery, the snow swallowed me. I pulled myself out of the deep banks by scaling a surrounding rock wall, like climbing an icy mountain. The tombstones rose like soft white bumps from the ground.

The ghosts sparkled in a small clearing ahead; three specters in the sun on crosses of snow.

I ran to the clearing, my heart pounding.

My foot hit a buried stump and I sank to my knees in the crusty ice and snow. The .357 jammed into my side. I pulled myself out and brushed the flakes from my eyes.

I didn't want to touch the ghosts, but I knew I had to find out the truth.

I raised myself up and stood before the middle cross. I carved a line with my finger from the top of the icy mound about half way down and some of the slick hardness fell away.

The face was gone, but I knew.

The agony of a death smile. Bits of bone and black hair.

I screamed into the forest, but no one heard except a tiny gray bird which fluttered away in a flurry of snow.

I listened.

A series of chirps and then silence.

The wind brushed against the pines.

"Oh, God, don't let it be," I prayed, the tears coming fast. "Oh, God. . . ."

Invocations were unnecessary. It was to be.

I furrowed my hand deeper into the crust, until the hard shell of ice split in half.

The bullet I had given him, still on the rawhide strap, was frozen to his sternum.

I took off my glove and touched the round black pellet. It was so cold my fingers nearly froze to it. But as I sat, huddled next to Stephen, warmth traveled through me like a slow fire. It was the oddest feeling, as if the love from his soul had touched mine. I wept and then shivered uncontrollably on the frozen ground.

When I returned to the cabin, I found a cellular phone but the battery was dead.

I took another look at Hugh. I wanted to sit his hideous corpse up and fire into it again and again until there was nothing left but frozen little pieces. I moved closer to study this man who had killed my friend and at least five others. Beside Hugh's body, I found Stephen's billfold.

Hugh's raised fist was locked and tight, but it held something between the bony fingers. I was able to get it out easily because it was cupped between his thumb and disintegrated palm.

I read the writing on the paper. I laughed and then I cried.

Stephen's name was written on the back of Rodney Jessup's card. There was also an address, 383 Putnam, Apt. 2, New Haven, and a phone number. "Hercules" was written in the upper left corner and a ghostly graphite fingerprint lay in the lower right.

The proof Stephen needed.

The proof he could have used to spoil Rodney Jessup's political ambitions.

The proof he carried with him to the end.

"Jesus, Des, what's wrong?" Ann Land asked.

The sun was setting behind the mountain and it was getting dark fast.

"Can I use your phone? I've got money for the call."

"Don't be silly. Be our guest." She lifted the phone to the counter.

The cat rubbed against my coat.

I dialed the number in Boston and John answered the phone.

I couldn't go on past "Hello."

"Des?" John fumbled with the phone. "Des, talk to me. Please. What's wrong?"

We were both crumbling and we both understood why.
A scream shot through the line and then there was silence.
Peace at last.

CHAPTER

TWENTY-TWO

I MISSED STEPHEN'S MEMORIAL SERVICE LATE December in Boston. I didn't have the heart for eulogies, the goodness, the praying, the crying, the final resolution. In my way, I had let go of Stephen the afternoon I came down from Hugh's cabin and called John.

There was another reason as well: I wasn't sure I had the courage to stand the pain of losing someone I loved. One of Stephen's traits that I admired—among others—was his courage. Stephen stuck his nose into everything. It took courage to delve into other people's business. I knew courage could be as simple as getting out of bed in the morning, or as instantaneous as the hero's rescue of the child in the burning building. But Stephen displayed it daily. He took on causes that few championed, defied groups that the less courageous mentioned only in a whisper.

The pain of his death brought me back to the time I had saved his life. He was standing outside a bar minding his own business when he was stabbed. From that point on, he was my friend and my fantasy lover—especially after I was shot by Ms. Deranged.

His visits to my hospital room cheered me and gave me hope that I might find my own love someday.

The service was held in a large gay friendly church on Arlington Street. I read in a gay rag that more than 500 people filled the sanctuary. Afterwards, Stephen's parents and John walked across the street to the Public Garden and spread a portion of Stephen's ashes near the large Japanese urn by the footbridge. I imagined them standing like black tombstones outlined against the snow, sprinkling the gray powder on the white ground.

Before he left Boston, John was driving to Provincetown to scatter the rest of the ashes at Herring Cove beach, a place they both loved.

Good night, sweet Prince: and flights of angels sing thee to thy rest.

A few months after Stephen's funeral, the city closed the Déjà Vu. The Zone was dying. The sexual heart of the city had suffered cardiac arrest for a parking lot.

The police constructed the end of Stephen's life at Hugh Mather's cabin. I constructed my own.

Stephen carried Rodney Jessup's card because he had loved him those many years ago. He had told me he couldn't find it because it was filed away, but he did find it (or had it all along) and was keeping it as his trump card. Perhaps he was going to turn it over to Chris Spinetti and didn't get the chance, or, just as likely, release it to the media after he "outed" Jessup. It would be a legitimate question to ask how Stephen could "out" a man he loved. I think time's distancing effect and the hard realization that Rodney was a completely different person led him to that decision. Not that Stephen didn't love John, or, in my fantasies, me, as well. In the end, Stephen's brush with fame got the better of him. He had to decide between love and hate and he hadn't accounted for the fortified armor worn by Rodney Jessup. He thought he could get through to the core of that young man from Virginia he'd met nearly twenty years before in a porn theater in New York City. Stephen tried and failed.

Hugh Mather apparently acted alone. Hugh was a former member of Aryan America, but there was no reason to believe that Carl Roy, or anyone else in the group, had ordered Hugh to commit the killings. Of course, in their way, through their hate, they had. Except for some intense media scrutiny after Stephen's body and the others were recovered, Carl and Aryan America escaped unscathed.

The day I dropped in on him, Carl must have thought long and hard about whether to call the police, not being one to have state and local authorities crawl over his property. I'm glad he did because his indecision, or efforts to cover up anything illegal, aided my escape. However, he must have been pretty convinced I was the Combat Zone Killer. Maybe he saw my capture as an opportunity to enhance his image, or get an embarrassing situation off his shoulders. I may have imagined Chris Spinetti's voice that night as I escaped from Adam; on the other hand, Carl may have had a handle on the Combat Zone killings and put two-and-two together in his misguided addition. At any rate, I never thought to ask Chris on our final night in the Déjà Vu if he had been on my trail in New Hampshire. Chris may have had time to make the trip from Boston, but I doubted he had much knowledge about the group other than his knowledge of Stephen's investigations. Chris wrote Aryan America on Stephen's computer screen because it made the most sense.

That left one question unanswered: How did Chris Spinetti know that Stephen had been kidnapped the evening of his speech? Unless he was working with Hugh, he didn't. I figured Chris had jumped at the opportunity to launch his blackmail scheme, not knowing whether Stephen might show up back at his apartment minutes or hours later. Either way, it wouldn't have made much difference. If Stephen returned early, Chris could claim that he was checking up on him and noticed that the apartment had been broken into. If Stephen showed up later, no one would have been the wiser because Chris, by then, would have covered his tracks and gotten at least some of the information he was looking for. Unfortunately for Chris, John and I happened to interrupt him as he was doing his dirty work. He never got the incriminating business card.

The death threats against Stephen remained unsolved, at least in my understanding. I'm sure Carl Roy would vehemently deny he ever offered half-a-million-dollars for the death of Stephen Cross. He may have been bankrolled, but not to that tune. Maybe one of Carl's men decided he was going to play a little joke on Stephen. Maybe Stephen made the threats up to get the attention of Rodney Jessup, or maybe Jessup decided to put the fear of God in Stephen by having one of his followers threaten him. Who knew? Certainly not the police. It was a moot point now.

So, the case of the Combat Zone Killer was closed. By all accounts, I was in the clear, but I still shied away from the police. I kept the SS dagger and the bullet that hung around Stephen's neck. They were the only souvenirs I had from a life cut short.

After Stephen's body was found, Rodney Jessup filed election papers in his run for the presidency.

I was sure no one knew that Chris Spinetti had attempted to blackmail Jessup. But I knew and I had Stephen's card.

For a time, I was undecided about what to do with the business card and Stephen's diary. I knew Stephen's words would devastate John, but I figured they might also become an outlet for John's rage. The more I thought about it, the more I realized I couldn't withhold these critical pieces of Stephen's life. John needed to know the truth despite the pain he might suffer. I mailed them to him, saying he could use the information any way he liked. He could report it all to the police or keep it to himself. I had been tempted to drop them off at the *New York Times* with a long letter, but I decided that wasn't in the best interests of Stephen's memory. At any rate, I would take great pride in derailing Jessup's campaign from afar, especially if the wreck was planned by John. Stephen was dead and I was certain Rodney assumed that his run for the presidency was assured. Something had to be done.

John could decide Stephen and Rodney's final fate.

I waited for the balloon to burst.

* * *

Desdemona: *Your wife, my lord; your true and loyal wife.*

Othello: *Come swear it. Damn thyself lest, being like one of heaven, the devils themselves should fear to seize thee: therefore be double damn'd: swear thou art honest.*

In the spring, I lingered over coffee at a shop on 47th Street. The street shimmered with the wet lights of cars and cabs. The morning, gray and oppressive with low-hanging clouds, dripped rain.

It had been nearly a year since Stephen Cross showed up at my apartment in Boston while Danny slept in my bed. My life had changed drastically since that time. Trauma always alters the psychological landscape of its victims, even those on the periphery.

Some early riser had left a copy of the *Times* on the counter. Two stories caught my eye—one was on the front page, the other buried inside. I put the paper down and considered whether my time in New York was up.

The murder of two gay men in Washington, D.C. was inside copy. They stripped them, dragged them through a grove of trees at Rock Creek, tied their hands behind their backs and shot each three times in the head.

My gift of prophecy divined the reason for these killings. They were murdered for silence. I'm not political—not a Republican, nor a Democrat, nor a member of any of the other parties or movements in America. I've never even voted in an election; but I am, in ways that other people are not, a man of action. Because of Stephen's death, I am acutely aware of actions and their consequences.

The headline on the front page screamed at me.

JESSUP SEX SCANDAL DEEPENS

I gratefully acknowledge the support and encouragement of Gordon Weissman, Mike Pecenka, Jim Linthwaite, Richard Hoffman, Leslie Lombino Schulz, CD Collins, Peter Brown, and the writers of The Writers' Room of Boston, where most of this book was written. I must thank my excellent beta readers, Bob Pinsky and Michael Grenier. I could not have completed this book without their astute insights. Thanks also should be given to Alyssa Maxwell; Evan Marshall, my agent; and the staff of Cleis Press for their guidance and support.